He stood close. So

She needed to move. [...] holding her breath, w[...] her. Was she a hypocrite for wa[...]

She licked her lips to keep from appearing too nervous. Or too eager?

His eyes dipped toward her mouth. "I'm waiting."

"For what?" For her?

"Waiting to hear you tell me what I did wrong to make you sneak out last night."

Hannah squeezed her eyes shut, not wanting to envision everything he'd done right that night. Her whisper came out on a soft breath. "Nothing. My son had a bad dream. I had to get him."

"I would've gone with you. Why didn't you wake me?"

"I don't want him taking this hero-worship thing too far."

"But I make such a good hero. After all, I rescued you that night, didn't I?" He pulled her close and traced her lip.

And that was when she knew she was in trouble. Because it wasn't just her son's heart she needed to protect from Isaac Jones.

* * *

AMERICAN HEROES:
They're coming home—and finding love!

Dear Reader,

The Firefighter's Christmas Reunion is extra special to me because it involves a second chance at love. My husband and I first met in our early twenties, but the timing wasn't right and Mr. Jeffries will tell anyone who'll listen that I broke his heart. Then, a few years later, I was in my last semester of law school and began visualizing my future. My thoughts kept coming back to that nice guy I'd once dated and, with a little encouragement from my friends, I called 4-1-1 (like we did before Google) and found his mom's home number.

Mr. Jeffries will also tell anyone who'll listen that I pursued him the second time around. But really, all it took was one message (and maybe a warning from his mom about guarding his heart) and he was calling me back less than two hours later. Sometimes things don't work out but every once in a while, we're lucky enough to get another shot.

After being gone for two years, Hannah Gregson returns to town to find her ex-boyfriend has moved back and is now the chief of the Sugar Falls Fire Department. Isaac Jones remembers their breakup a little differently, yet he wants to think he's moved on from that summer after high school. Unfortunately, it's difficult to put their pasts behind them when they're constantly faced with so many memories...

For more information on my other Harlequin Special Edition books, visit my website at christyjeffries.com, or chat with me on Twitter, @christyjeffries. You can also find me on Facebook and Instagram. I'd love to hear from you.

Happy Holidays,

Christy Jeffries

The Firefighter's Christmas Reunion

Christy Jeffries

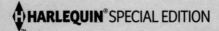

Recycling programs
for this product may
not exist in your area.

ISBN-13: 978-1-335-46617-4

The Firefighter's Christmas Reunion

Copyright © 2018 by Christy Jeffries

Printed in U.S.A.

www.Harlequin.com

Christy Jeffries graduated from the University of California, Irvine, with a degree in criminology, and received her juris doctor from California Western School of Law. But drafting court documents and working in law enforcement was merely an apprenticeship for her current career in the dynamic field of mommyhood and romance writing. She lives in Southern California with her patient husband, two energetic sons and one sassy grandmother. Follow her online at christyjeffries.com.

Visit the Author Profile page at Harlequin.com.

To Francie Freetly Huttner—
my favorite mother-in-law, an adoring grammie
and the life of every party. Becoming your daughter
has been a wonderful blessing and I hope that
I always make you proud. Also, thank you for not
deleting my voice mail when I called your house
sixteen years ago looking for your son...

Chapter One

Chief Isaac Jones commanded the stainless steel griddle in the kitchen of the Grange Hall the same way he did the Sugar Falls Fire Station—with a steady hand and a slight wonder that he'd ended up in this position in the first place.

Flipping a row of pancakes, he caught the flash of a blue shirt and gold neckerchief out of the corner of his eye. "Hey, partner," Isaac said to one of the young Cub Scouts balancing three loaded paper plates between two small hands. "Can you find Mister Jonesy out there and tell him we're gonna need more batter?"

"We're almost out of syrup, too," the chief of police, who also happened to be the pack leader for Troop 1307, said from the pass-through window separating the kitchen from the rows of tables and chairs set up in the main room. "I'll run to Duncan's Market and grab everything they have on their shelves."

"I knew I should've ordered all the supplies before I left," Isaac mumbled to no one in particular. It might be the last Saturday of October, but Sugar Falls was experiencing an unprecedented heat wave, and the unusually high temperatures meant nobody wanted to linger in the overheated kitchen this morning. When he'd originally volunteered the fire department to cosponsor the Scouts' pancake breakfast fundraiser, he hadn't anticipated that the National Guard would move his unit's annual two-week training up an entire month. Which meant that he hadn't been in Sugar Falls ordering supplies for today.

"What can I do to help?" someone asked over the whirling of the industrial fan behind him.

The back of Isaac's neck tingled at the familiar sound of the woman's voice. His breathing stuttered. He hadn't seen her in over ten years, and last he'd heard, she was joining the Peace Corps or a similar outfit volunteering in Africa somewhere. So surely it couldn't be…

His dread was confirmed the second he turned around. Hannah Gregson.

His lungs refused to draw air for at least ten seconds as she stood there, her blond hair twisted into a messy knot and her proud shoulders pushed back as though she was ready to take on the world's problems. She didn't wear an ounce of makeup, but her complexion was as pure and fresh as it had been the summer after their senior year of high school.

"Your pancakes are burning," she said, grabbing the spatula out of his clenched hand and easily swinging her tall, lithe body in front of his to scoop the blackened circles off the griddle.

Had she not recognized him?

Sure, Isaac had filled out a bit since he was eighteen, and he no longer sported the longer, fuller curls he'd worn in his youth. In fact, his hair was more of a fade now, a shorter style he'd grown accustomed to when he'd joined the Army after college. But he hadn't changed *that* much.

Of course, the last time she'd seen Isaac was the night of that Labor Day bonfire and neither one of them had been at their finest.

He cleared his throat. "What are you doing here?"

"Making pancakes?" She tossed a cheeky smile over her shoulder. It was then that recognition finally dawned in her pale blue eyes and he experienced a tiny rush of satisfaction that she appeared to be as thrown off by his presence as he was by hers. "Isaac?"

"What's this about you needing more batter?" Uncle Jonesy asked as he strode into the kitchen at that exact second. The old cowboy took one look at Hannah and said, "Aw, hell."

"Hi, Jonesy," Hannah said, lifting the spatula in a feeble wave. Good. At least she was now aware of the uneasiness circling the confines of this kitchen.

Jonesy was quick to recover, though, because he stepped around the stainless steel worktable in the center of the room and lifted Hannah up into a big bear hug. She let out a surprised squeak and Isaac's uncle chuckled. "I heard you were back in town, hon."

Isaac's eyebrows shot to his hairline. He had? It would've been nice if the old man had given him a heads-up.

"I just got back a couple of weeks ago," she said, and Isaac realized that Hannah must've arrived right after he'd left for his Guard training. He hooked his thumbs into his pockets, aiming for a casualness he didn't feel as he studied her. They never had been able to stay around each other long enough to make things work.

"I bet your mama and daddy are excited you're finally back in Idaho." Jonesy smiled.

The Gregsons were originally from Boise. Summer kids, like Isaac, who only visited Sugar Falls during the warm months when they were out on school break. After he moved into the dorms at Yale, he'd heard through the grapevine that Hannah had decided to save money by going to Boise State, which must've been a real coincidence since Carter Mahoney was also attending that school on a full ride track-and-field scholarship. After hearing that she'd also gone home with Carter for Thanksgiving that same year, Isaac had made it a point to avoid any conversations that had to do with Hannah Gregson and where she was living. Or who she was seeing.

After ten years, he certainly didn't want to hear about it now. Rocking back onto the heels of his work boots, Isaac heard the annoyance in his own voice when he asked, "Are you two gonna sit around and catch up or are we going to make some pancakes?"

"Guess I'll run out and try to wrangle us some more mix." His uncle's gaze shifted between them as he scrubbed the gray whiskers on his ruddy face, probably eager to beat a hasty retreat. Deserter.

"Then I'll get started on another bowl of batter." Hannah passed the spatula to Isaac, her long, slender fingers coming into contact with his palm. A heat that had nothing to do with the nearby empty griddle spread through his gut.

"You don't need to help." Isaac's tone came out more harsh and dismissive than he'd intended. "What I mean is that the fire department and the Scouts are putting the breakfast on. So we don't really need any outside volunteers."

"Hmm." She looked around the empty kitchen. "It appears that you're rather short-staffed at the moment."

Okay, so that was slightly true. But he'd rather have no staff than have a bossy do-gooder like Hannah Gregson near him. Her mere presence echoed everything that his venture capitalist mother had drilled into him as a kid. Being an African American woman married to an older white investment banker, Isaac's mom constantly had to prove herself at her husband's bank before launching her own private equity firm and taking the biotech world by storm. Whether it was a grade at the science fair or a game at the county fair, his mother always insisted that her only child be better than the best.

Maybe that ingrained competitiveness was why Hannah's intrinsic need to lead by example had always come across as a challenge to Isaac.

And today was no different.

"I'm only on my own temporarily," he defended. "My crew is responding to a call at the elementary school."

She gasped and he quickly held up his free palm, the one that wasn't still tingling from her earlier touch. "Don't worry. It's the thirteenth time they've been out there this weekend. The district went with a low-bid contractor to install the new fire detection system. Most likely it's another false alarm and they'll be back in ten minutes."

Hannah's mouth relaxed, but her eyes sparkled with determination. "Then I can fill in for them in the meantime."

With the growing number of young Scouts lining up at the pass-through window waiting for more plates of pancakes to serve, Isaac had to admit that he could use another hand. He studied her slender, strong fingers knotting the apron strings in front of her flat stomach. He just wasn't quite sure he was ready for *her* hands.

Isaac cleared his throat. "Thanks for offering, but I'm sure one of the kids' parents can come back here and help us."

"I *am* one of the parents," she replied, and Isaac's heart slammed into his rib cage.

"Huh?" He must've looked as confused as he felt because Hannah rolled her eyes and jerked a thumb toward the dining area.

"My son's a Cub Scout and his entire den is out there right now, wondering if these pancakes are going to cook themselves."

"You have a son?"

Hannah could see Isaac Jones's hazel eyes shifting back and forth as his brain made calculations. She hadn't seen the man in ten years—since before he became a man, really—but some habits were hard to break and she could clearly see that his penchant for jumping to wrong conclusions was one of them. "Yes. His name is Samuel."

"Is he…? I mean, uh…how old is your…um, son?" Isaac stammered. No doubt that he was expecting the age to coincide with the date they'd last been together and Hannah wondered if the guy's ego knew no bounds.

Of course, with those wide shoulders and that perfectly warm brownskin with bronze undertones, he was definitely handsome enough to have an ego.

Instead of answering, though, she focused her trembling hands on the task of opening up the only box of pancake mix she could find and dumping it into a stainless steel bowl. After the way Isaac had once broken her trust and her heart, he didn't even deserve to ask her about the weather, let alone such a personal question.

But her enjoyment at letting him squirm was short-lived because Sammy came into the kitchen at that exact moment. Hannah's heart melted at her six-year-old's hesitant steps and his round, wide eyes under the stiff blue cap. Straightening his gold neckerchief, she quietly asked, "How's it going out there?"

Sammy tugged at her apron and Hannah bent down so she could hear his whispery, soft voice. "Those people sure eat a lot."

"I know." Hannah stroked a hand along the boy's smooth ebony cheek. She'd read all the books and talked to countless other families about the transitioning effects of cross-cultural adoptions and children relocating overseas, especially for a child who had spent most of his life in a village orphanage in Ghana until he'd moved into a small cottage on the same premises with Hannah. "But don't worry. We will have plenty of food for everyone. Do you want to help me mix up more pancakes?"

"No, thank you," her son replied a bit more loudly, his accent making him sound almost British. "Uncle Luke said I could help him count out the change in the box. My cousins told me I need to learn how much the coins are worth so that the other kids at school won't steal my lunch money and buy pudding cups with it."

Hannah scrunched her nose. Her twin nephews were already proving to be a horrible influence on Sammy. But at least the nine-year-olds were coaxing the shy boy out of his shell and attempting to protect their newest family member. She gave his shoulder a reassuring squeeze and tried to ignore Isaac's blatant stare from the other side of the kitchen as Sammy walked out, only slightly more confident than he'd been when he entered.

"Was that your son?" Isaac asked, his voice even

deeper and smoother than it had been when they were teenagers.

Stiffening her spine as straight as it would go, she turned to confront the man she'd stupidly fallen for all those years ago.

"I adopted him while I was in Africa on a Teachers Without Borders program."

He slowly nodded and she watched the relief drain over his face. Then one side of his full lips quirked up, immediately reminding her body of the way his mischievous smile had always had the ability to draw her in. "So you became a teacher after all."

Hannah grunted, choking down her outrage. How dare he take pride in the memory of their late-night talks sitting on the tailgate of his Uncle Jonesy's old, rusted-out pickup truck? The conversations where she'd told him about her ambitions and her dreams and he'd told her that she was going to make the world a better place. She cracked an egg so hard, half the shell fell into her mixing bowl.

Luckily, she was saved from having to make any further casual small talk when his uncle swung through the door, balancing a sack of pancake mix in each gnarled hand. "Look what I found! No thanks to Freckles over at the Cowgirl Up Café, mind you. That ol' gal cursed me up and down a blue streak for not knowin' that her flapjacks were made from scratch."

"So then where'd you get these?" Isaac stepped away from the stove to relieve Jonesy of half his load.

"One of the ladies from that quilting group over at the community church brought them over, saying we could borrow theirs as long as we replace it before their homeless outreach breakfast next week."

Hannah wanted to ask if they'd had a sudden outpour-

ing of homeless people relocating to the touristy mountain town of Sugar Falls. When she'd left two years ago,
there'd been a handful of regulars stopping by the shelter for an occasional hot meal, but that was usually only
in the snowy, winter months.

However, she kept her lips firmly clamped, not sure if
she was ready to find out what else had changed around
here since she'd been gone.

As she whisked, Isaac turned to the stove and she
tried not to peek at his back. He'd always had those slim
hips and long legs, but when had his shoulders gotten so
broad? Probably around the same time that his jawline
had gotten more chiseled.

Stop it, she commanded herself. This tingling sensation under her skin wasn't because she was still attracted
to Isaac, it was simply her body's way of responding to
the shock of seeing him after all these years. In fact, she
hadn't even recognized him at first. Maybe because she'd
been so successful at blocking out all thoughts of the one
guy who'd ever broken her heart.

Of course, his curls were gone and his hair was now
cropped close. Plus, Hannah never would have expected
to see him wearing pants, since she'd only spent time
with him during the summer months. Actually, it was
a bit jarring *not* to see him in a pair of board shorts and
dressed in a shirt with sleeves that hadn't been cut off.
What wasn't unusual, though, was to see him in a Sugar
Falls Fire Department tee since his uncle had always run
the volunteer department.

Why hadn't anyone in her family warned her that Isaac
was visiting this fall? Not that her brothers didn't have
their own busy lives, but they should've known that she
would want some advance notice that she might run into
her ex-boyfriend. While they'd both joined the Navy two

years before that fateful summer, they had to have seen the grainy footage of that video someone had taken of Isaac and then posted on the internet.

Her body shuddered at the suppressed memory. Despite the fact that it had been taken down twenty-four hours later, everybody had seen it. The entire town had heard his recorded accusations and she'd never been in such a hurry to return home to Boise.

In fact, after college, Hannah had initially hesitated to take the teaching position in Sugar Falls. She only accepted when she'd been convinced that all the gossip about her had died down. It'd helped knowing that during Isaac's irate monologue online, he'd told the person holding the video camera that he was leaving for good and would never come back to Idaho for as long as he lived.

Looked like that was another promise Isaac Jones had broken.

Channeling all the old hurt into her whisk, Hannah made bowl after bowl of pancake batter, refusing to think about the man standing only a few feet away from her. She kept her attention focused on the pass-through window and on the boys approaching in their Scout uniforms. She hoped Sammy was fitting in with them and wasn't overwhelmed by all the new faces. Maybe she shouldn't have signed him up for extracurricular activities so soon. But he'd be starting a brand new school on Monday and she knew how rough the first day could be for a transfer student who was already accustomed to American schools. It would be twice as awkward for her son.

After a tense hour of Hannah and Isaac each pretending that the other wasn't there, Sammy rushed into the kitchen wearing a big grin, revealing two missing teeth. "We made four hundred and twenty-eight dollars. How much is that in cedis?"

Hannah had an app on her smartphone that would con-
vert US dollars into Ghanaian currency, but she couldn't
remember where she'd left her purse. She was about to
say as much to Sammy when she heard an older boy in a
tan Scout uniform snicker. "That's worth two goats and
a water buffalo where you come from."

Anger flooded her and she was about to admonish
the mean-spirited kid when Isaac called out, "Hey, JP,
since you seem to know so much about livestock, why
don't you go help Scooter Deets fill up those slop buck-
ets he brought over from his ranch. He needs someone
to sort through the trash for any leftover pancake bits
that might've gotten thrown out. I'm sure his hogs will
appreciate it."

"But that's disgusting," the bigger boy said. "Those
trash bags are covered in syrup and junk."

Isaac's only response was a steely scowl that didn't
invite any more back talk. Hannah should learn how to
imitate that expression, since it might prove useful in her
classroom full of fifth-graders this school year. JP pivoted with a huff, muttering under his breath as he shoved
past a smirking eight-year-old who hid a box of plastic
gloves behind his back. Apparently her son wasn't the
only boy who'd been picked on by this bully.

"Kids like that are jealous of worldly guys like us."
Isaac finally turned toward Sammy and gave him a wink.
Worldly? Maybe. But *guys like us*? Please. As if her ex-
boyfriend was anything like her sweet son. However,
before Hannah could say as much, the man continued.
"When I was younger and first came to Sugar Falls to
visit my Uncle Jonesy, some of the other boys in town
didn't know what to think because I was new and different. But my uncle kept a close watch to make sure nobody

messed with me. So if JP gives you any more problems, let me know and I'll set him straight."

"I will." Sammy nodded as he approached Isaac, curiosity apparent in his expression.

Hannah felt her heels press back onto the ground, her calf muscles relaxing as the fight drained out of her. It wasn't like she could get mad at the person who'd just defended her son. Then again, it was *her* role as Sammy's mother to be his number one protector. After all, it wasn't like Isaac would be around in the future to take on all the bullies of the world.

"Why are you making them so fat?" her son asked as Isaac poured the last of the batter onto the griddle.

"What do you mean, big guy?" Isaac asked, and Hannah tried to steel her heart against the sweet tone of his voice. Sammy was a few inches shorter and much thinner than the other six-year-olds in his den. So his smile lit up even more at being referred to as *big guy*.

"In Ghana, our pancakes are real skinny. Like pieces of paper."

Isaac knelt down to speak to the boy and Hannah strained to hear his reply. "I'll tell you what. If you get the recipe for me, next time we have a pancake breakfast, we'll make them your way. I had some like that once when I lived in Morocco and I bet everyone in town will love 'em."

Something tugged low in Hannah's belly. Isaac hadn't said that he'd make Sammy his own batch, which would only have made her son feel more different and out of place. Instead, he'd had the perfect response, offering to bring a piece of Sammy's old life to share with everyone in his new life.

It was too bad Isaac Jones never kept his word.

Chapter Two

The strident bell pierced Hannah's eardrums and she frantically looked around the classroom for her son, who'd been helping her staple the words Happy Halloween to the bulletin board that had belonged to Mrs. Fernandez before the teacher had gone on maternity leave. Sammy dropped the stapler and had his hands covering his own ears. His pupils were wide but, thankfully, not filled with terror.

"It's just the fire alarm," she told him, using her calmest teacher voice. "Come on. I'll show you where we line up."

She reached for his hand and, though his expression was filled with a mix of curiosity and tension, he immediately latched onto Hannah and followed her out to the nearly empty hallway lined with student artwork from earlier this year. His head pivoted in every possible direction and he asked, "Where is the fire?"

"There probably isn't a fire, sweetie. Otherwise, we'd

smell the smoke. My bet is they're just testing the alarm to make sure it works." A few other teachers—who, like her, must've come in on a Sunday to catch up on lesson plans and grading—trickled out of various rooms and toward the front door. Some of the tension left Sammy's fingers as he saw that nobody else was concerned about the constant peal of the bell. Hannah raised her voice to be heard over it, as well as the siren on the fire engine pulling into the drop-off lane. "At the beginning of the school year, the teachers show all the kids what we do during a fire drill. But since we're both coming in a little late this semester, we'll get to figure it out together."

It might've sounded like a grand adventure, except Hannah was pretty sure she hadn't yet explained about fire drills to Sammy. Actually, there was a lot she hadn't explained to the boy, but she hadn't wanted to overwhelm him with information. There'd been classrooms at the children's home where he'd lived and he was excited about attending school. Although he had an accent from growing up in the Western region of Ghana, the orphanage had been founded by British missionaries. There wouldn't be much of a language barrier, just a cultural one. Besides, he was a smart child. Not everything was new and different, so there was no need to be patronizing. Her plan was to stick close to him and try to explain things as he experienced them for the first time.

Hannah basked in the sheer awe on her son's face as she realized that this was the first time Sammy had seen an American fire engine up close. But that shared excitement gave way to an unexpected wobble in Hannah's stomach.

Speaking of firsts, she'd also never before witnessed the sight of Isaac Jones in turnout gear. Well, at least, in the yellow pants and red suspenders. It was still unseasonably warm and neither he nor the other three people exiting the huge red truck wore their jackets.

Whoa. It was bad enough that he'd broken his vow to never visit Sugar Falls again, but since when did the city allow tourists to ride around in the fire engine? Not that he was a typical tourist.

Still. Isaac had been a summer kid, like her, and since it was now closing in on November, it should be well past time for him to be going back to…where? Where did he live now?

Mrs. Dunn, the school nurse, bustled past a stunned Hannah and greeted the firefighters. "Sorry you guys had to come out again, Chief. I thought the alarm company had fixed everything yesterday."

Who was she calling *chief*? Certainly not Isaac. Grabbing onto the metal handrail on the stairs in front of the school, Hannah racked her brain for the slightest scrap of recollection about their brief, and extremely awkward, conversation yesterday morning in the Grange Hall kitchen. Last night, she'd gone over every word, facial expression and movement he'd made that day. Had she missed something?

The blue T-shirt he was wearing was very similar to the one he'd had on at the pancake breakfast. The one she'd assumed he'd gotten from his uncle who led the volunteer crew. Although, this time, Hannah's eyes zeroed in on the words Chief Jones stenciled in white letters over one of his well-formed pectoral muscles.

Oh. No.

Isaac paused only for a second when his gaze landed on her. If Hannah hadn't already been gawking at him, she would've missed it. But he was quick to recover and turned all of his attention toward Nurse Dunn. "You might want to call them out again. In the meantime, have everyone stay here while we go make sure the building is clear."

Hannah's palms were cool and clammy, which must've made it easy for Sammy's fingers to slip out of her hand. Before she could pry her stunned mouth open and stop him, he was bounding down the stairs and sprinting toward Isaac.

She should've expected it. Her son loved big trucks and he loved running every time he got the chance. But she was still in a state of shock.

"Can I come with you?" Sammy asked, further surprising Hannah. Her son normally didn't warm up to people very quickly and he was always way too shy to ask for what he wanted.

Isaac smiled at the boy and bent down. "Not right this second, big guy. But as soon as we make sure that there isn't a fire inside, I can let you climb up into the engine and pull the switch for the siren." The man's hazel gaze flickered over Hannah and he amended, "If you're still here when we come out."

She sucked air through her clenched teeth. What was that supposed to mean? Did Isaac think she was just going to run off at the mere sight of him? If so, he had another thought coming. She marched down the steps and recaptured Sammy's hand, forcing a tense smile at her son, but refusing to make eye contact with Isaac. "We can wait."

The truth was, she couldn't leave, even if she wanted to. Her purse and car keys were still inside her classroom. Two teachers she'd known from her previous years at the elementary school were huddled with the nurse on the front sidewalk. However, their whispering stopped when Hannah looked their way. Not that she could blame them for their curiosity at seeing one of their recently returned coworkers suddenly confronted with the reappearance of an old flame. But it still made Hannah's nerves twist.

She let out a sigh when Sammy tugged on her hand, pulling her closer to check out the fire engine. While she definitely did not share her son's enthusiasm for the monstrous vehicle that had brought her ex-boyfriend literally screeching back into her life, at least Hannah now had an excuse to avoid any conversations where she might be asked about why her skin had gone as red as the truck the second Isaac appeared.

Unfortunately, her relief was short-lived because the incessantly loud ringing came to a sudden halt. In fact, in the echo of the fire alarm's silence, she could hear her pulse picking up tempo. That meant Isaac was coming back this way and now it was Hannah's internal alarm bells going off.

"All clear," one of the other firefighters—the driver—announced and Hannah was surprised to see that Nurse Dunn and the other two teachers had already left. Hannah's car was the only one remaining in the lot and she again silently cursed herself for not bringing her purse and keys with her. The female firefighter came out next and Hannah found herself hoping that one of them could quickly show Sammy the fire engine so they could sneak back to her classroom before Isaac arrived.

But there was no such luck. Isaac, looking way more confident and smug than he had a right to, came loping down the steps. He passed a clipboard to the fourth firefighter and said, "Write up the report, Rook. I have a junior officer here who needs to learn how to drive the engine."

Isaac gave Sammy a high five and then the boy sprinted after him toward the driver's side of the big red truck.

"No problem, Chief," the baby-faced young man said before smiling at Hannah. She looked at his nametag. Clausson. He didn't look familiar to her. In fact, she realized as she scanned the other firefighters' faces, she didn't know any of them.

"Apparently, the volunteer fire department is finally recruiting people under the age of fifty-five." Hannah's forced chuckle sounded more like a nervous giggle and the younger man lifted one dark eyebrow at her.

"Don't worry. Jonesy and Scooter and the rest of the elders are still around picking up volunteer shifts. But now that the city also has a paid department, our full-time crews are a bit…oh, shall we say…less seasoned." Clausson gave her a wink, but her heart was already rioting inside her chest, so it didn't have the flirtatious effect he might've intended.

"You mean you're not a volunteer?" she asked, though she had a feeling she already knew the answer.

"None of us are today, miss."

So if Isaac wasn't a volunteer, this wasn't just some short-term gig for him. Which meant that he wasn't here temporarily. Hannah forced herself to breathe deeply. She was seriously going to throttle her older brothers for not warning her.

Young Clausson leaned closer and lowered his voice. "If you want to come by the brand-new station, I can arrange to give you, uh…a private tour."

"Hey, Rook." The female firefighter walked between them and tapped on Clausson's clipboard. "If the chief catches you putting the moves on his ex-girlfriend instead of writing that report, you're going to be on laundry detail indefinitely."

Clausson's whiskerless cheeks turned a shade of pink as he muttered a four-letter word and scrambled away so quickly that Hannah choked on the sudden cloud of over-powering cologne left in his wake.

Well, she was either choking on the scent, or on the female firefighter's unexpected statement. Hannah looked down at the woman's nametag—Rodriguez—then cleared her throat. "I'm not really Isaac's ex-girlfriend, you know."

"Sorry about that." Rodriguez transferred her helmet from one arm to the other and gave a sheepish grimace before extending her hand. "I'm Olivia. I've only lived here for eighteen months and I'm still learning how to navigate small-town gossip."

"Hannah Gregson," she swallowed, returning the handshake. "There's…uh…gossip? I mean, obviously there's gossip, but I just hadn't expected it already."

She was dying to ask what people were saying, but she closed her eyes and gave a brief shake of her head. Nope. Hannah didn't care back then what people thought and she certainly didn't care now.

"The talk is why I assumed something was going on between you two," Olivia explained and Hannah's fingers curled into her hipbones as she twisted the fabric inside her jeans' pockets.

"I guess, technically, we're exes, but it was more of a summer fling when we were in high school." She attempted a casual shrug but her shoulders were too stiff to properly execute it. "Maybe two summer flings. But it wasn't like we had an ongoing official status or anything since it was *strictly* only a part-time, seasonal kinda relationship. Really, things didn't get all that hot and heavy until *after* graduation…oh, my gosh, I need to stop talking."

Hannah pinched the bridge of her nose, squeezing her eyes shut so she wouldn't have to see Rodriguez's response to her long-winded ramblings. "Anyway, it was all so long ago, I hardly ever think about it anymore." She gave the woman a tense smile. "I should go check on my son."

Her legs were trembling with a combination of embarrassment and annoyance as she walked toward the cab of the fire engine. Embarrassment that she'd just spilled her guts to a complete stranger who also happened to work for Isaac. And annoyance because Hannah hadn't been better prepared to deal with suddenly having the man back in her life.

Watching the fire chief put his helmet on Sammy's head as her son held on to the huge steering wheel, pretending to drive the truck, she felt a wave of tenderness battle against the rest of her raging emotions. Unfortunately, her irritation won out and she her rib cage expanded with each frustrated breath.

Hannah had never expected that the arrogant, rich teenager she'd once known would leave his perfectly mapped-out life on the East Coast and return to Sugar Falls, let alone move here permanently.

And who in the world had thought it would be a good idea to put someone like him in charge of the fire department, responsible for saving innocent people?

Indifference would have been Isaac's first choice of reactions to seeing the woman who'd once held his teenage heart in her hands. Annoyance, or even anger, would also have been an expected response to seeing Hannah again, though, most of the aching bitterness he'd held on to throughout college had dissipated. Instead, Isaac found himself filled with a weird sort of curiosity about her and hadn't stopped thinking about her since she'd showed up yesterday. And the last thing he wanted was for someone—especially her—to mistake that curiosity for renewed interest. He'd had ten years to grow wiser and thicken his skin. There was no way he'd fall under her spell a second time.

He looked over Sammy's head at the woman standing on the opposite side of the cab of the fire engine, her lips twisted into a tight line while she eyeballed the two of them. Really, it wasn't as if he was going toss her son into a raging inferno the second she took her eyes off him. Would it hurt Hannah to take a step back and maybe not frown quite so much?

Her blond hair was twisted into another messy bun secured to the top of her head with two pencils, and Isaac had to admit that her face was still as striking as ever, with strong, high cheekbones and aqua blue eyes that never used to be so guarded. So wary. Scanning past her faded flannel work shirt and down the length of her, he noticed that her legs were still long and lean, but her hips were just a little fuller. Everything about her was the same, except more. More mature, more compelling, more…arousing.

"Can I turn on the siren?" Sammy's voice was soft and tentative, as though he was afraid to ask for what he wanted. Despite his reserved manner, amazement glowed out of the boy's eyes and Isaac knew the kid was a goner. Just like Isaac had been the first time he'd visited his Uncle Jonesy and toured the old volunteer station.

Isaac stayed with his uncle the summer after his parents' divorce and then returned every June through August after that. One would think that he and Hannah would've bonded over their status as "summer kids," but she was more of a social activist than a socializer. It wasn't until after they were sixteen that Little Miss Do-Gooder had come out of her shell and spoken more than a sentence to him at an impromptu car wash fundraiser she'd organized to raise money for a local animal shelter.

It was also the first time that he'd ever seen her in a bathing suit and he would never forget the way she'd—

"Sammy, we should probably let the firefighters get back to work," Hannah called through the open passenger door, interrupting Isaac's steamy memory.

"Okay." Her son's shoulders slumped, but he didn't let go of the steering wheel.

"Wait," she said quickly. "Would you guys mind if I took a picture of him sitting there with the helmet on and everything?"

Isaac was used to kids and their fascination with fire engines and uniforms, so it was a pretty standard request from a doting parent. He attempted a casual shrug before replying, "No problem."

She patted down her denim-clad hips before a blush stole up her cheeks. "I left my phone in the classroom."

A flurry of emotions crossed Hannah's face and Isaac could tell she was wrestling with whether to leave her precious son unattended with him or to forego the picture altogether. While Isaac hadn't exactly been proud of the way he'd handled their breakup all those years ago, Hannah surely had to know that he wasn't a complete monster. Even if he'd still been holding on to a ten-year-old grudge, which he clearly wasn't, Isaac would never involve an innocent child in a petty dispute. Anyone who knew him would know that.

However, Hannah obviously hadn't really known him back then and she certainly didn't know him now. Otherwise, she wouldn't always be expecting the worst from him. She wouldn't have been so quick to move on after that night...

Taking pity on the kid, Isaac reached into his pocket

and pulled out his own smartphone. He tapped on the camera icon before passing it through the cab of the truck. "Here, you can use mine."

As her pupils darted down to the electronic device and back up to him, the changing expression on her face suggested she was struggling to make a decision. Isaac couldn't help himself from adding, "Unless you have a better offer."

Narrowing her eyes, she reached out so quickly, her fingers brushed across the back of his hand. Although the brief contact was only the result of him purposely goading her, it was the second time in the past forty-eight hours that the slightest touch from Hannah had sent his pulse skyrocketing.

But her words quickly brought him back down to earth. "As I recall, you were never hurting for any offers yourself."

Isaac's brow twisted in confusion. What in the hell was that supposed to mean? And was it his imagination, or did the phone tremble slightly as she held it up to frame the image?

Hannah moved the phone forward and backward, then immediately lowered the screen, revealing her sucked-in cheeks. Isaac flashed back to a memory of her doing the same thing whenever she'd been embarrassed. But the sweet memory was soon replaced with a less pleasant sensation when she finally said, "Would you mind backing up?"

He looked at the steel step he was standing on outside the driver's side door. If he backed up any more, he'd be on the asphalt. His gaze returned to her and she gave him a tense nod, encouraging him to step down. "If you didn't want me in the picture, you could've just said so."

"I thought I did," she mumbled, then she jerked her

head toward Sammy with a pointed look that could only indicate that she was hoping to avoid any type of unpleasantness in front of her son.

She'd never been very good at confrontation, at least, not where Isaac had been concerned. And apparently she hadn't gotten much better. Not that he'd come here looking for a fight; however, there was only so much professional courtesy he could extend. Community outreach was part of his job, rehashing the past was not. Keeping his mouth firmly shut, he jumped down off the rig and tried to pretend that he didn't notice Hannah's obvious change in tone when she sweetly told her son to count to three and say cheese.

Chapter Three

"I can't believe you didn't tell me that he was back in town," Hannah said to her brother Luke as soon as Sammy ran out the back door to play with his older cousins.

"Who is *he*?" Carmen, her soon-to-be sister-in-law, asked as she set out a salad bowl full of mixed berries.

"Don't ask," her brother whispered to his fiancée.

"Isaac Jones!" Hannah might as well have shouted, her voice echoed so loudly inside the old Victorian home Luke's family had just moved into. He turned to the pizza boxes she'd set on the counter, but not before she caught his eye roll.

"You mean the fire chief?" Carmen asked, then gave Luke a reprimanding look and closed the cardboard lid on his hand. "You get the boys washed up. I'll set the table."

"What table?" Luke asked, looking out of the kitchen and into the empty dining room. "Hannah kept everything when she moved back into our cabin."

"First of all, you got Nana's Oldsmobile and I got all of her outdated furniture, which I lovingly and painfully refurbished before I went to Ghana," Hannah said slowly, as though she was explaining fairness to a first grader—for the eight hundredth time. "Secondly, it's the Gregson *family* cabin, and I lived there first."

"Ignore your brother." Carmen gave a dismissive wave. "He's wanted to live in town since he moved to Sugar Falls full time and when you got back, he finally had an excuse to buy this old fixer-upper. Anyway, do you and Chief Jones have history or something?"

"History? Ha!" Luke said around a mouthful of pepperoni he'd sneaked off one of the pizzas. "You guys were barely outta high school. Shouldn't you be over that by now?"

Carmen's eyes lit up. She was a cop, and Hannah had a feeling that she was dying to investigate something other than who was at fault for the latest fender bender in the Duncan's Market parking lot.

"Of course I'm over him," Hannah argued. Her head pounded and her arms ached from cutting out all of those pumpkin shapes from cardstock before stapling them to her new bulletin board. The first day back at school was always chaotic, but since she was coming into the classroom halfway through the semester, this year was already proving to be an uphill battle in concentration. She tried to remind herself that she'd been lucky to get this last-minute teaching assignment when she'd rushed home unexpectedly to be closer to her mom. Rubbing her temples, she added, "It's just that it would've been nice to be forewarned that I'd have to see him on a regular basis. I didn't even know that Sugar Falls had a real fire department now."

Luke gestured at his wife's blue uniform with a greasy

thumb. "As soon as the residents of Sugar Falls voted to form their own police force, everyone knew that a fire station was going to be next. They're even housed in the same building. On two separate sides, obviously."

Hannah sighed. Before she'd left for Ghana, she'd attended every school board and city council meeting there was. She should've expected as much and normally would be the first to endorse the improvement of their town. But did they have to hire Isaac Jones?

"What are his qualifications, anyway?" she muttered to herself, but Carmen's raised brow indicated she'd heard. "I mean, besides volunteering with his uncle and racing around town as if he had a siren permanently attached to anything he drove. Including that jet boat he used to drive way too fast on Rush Lake, showing off for all those girls from Sugar Falls High."

"I remember that boat! That's the one his dad bought him for his sixteenth birthday." Luke smiled, then caught his bride-to-be's eye and quickly cleared his throat. "I mean, I remember that it went fast. I don't exactly recall the part about the girls..."

Carmen laughed at Luke's flustered explanation. "Perhaps I should put on my bikini and grab a wakeboard to help jog your memory."

Luke pulled his fiancée toward him and whispered something in her ear, causing her to squeal with laughter.

Hannah rolled her eyes at the smitten couple. "I lived in this town for five years after college and didn't have so much as a blind date. I'm barely out of the country and you and Drew and every other single person in Sugar Falls are getting married off."

"Technically," Luke said, tapping his bare ring finger. "I'm still waiting for Carmen to make an honest man out of me."

"Good luck with that," Hannah said with a snort. Then she added, "How're the wedding plans going?"

"Moving the date up to Thanksgiving week was a little tricky. We had to switch venues, make it more of a destination wedding so that Carmen's family wouldn't have so far to travel. But the sooner we have it, the easier it will be for Mom to...you know."

The immediate silence grounded Hannah and reminded her that she had bigger issues to address in her life than the reappearance of Isaac Jones. Nobody had really brought up their mother's recent diagnosis, as though to mention the cancer would cause it to spread more quickly.

The old house creaked and a shed door slammed shut outside, highlighting the uncomfortable quiet that had suddenly settled between the three of them. Finally, Carmen said, "I was hoping you'd be one of my bridesmaids."

Hannah practically sighed, grateful to have the subject changed back to something more pleasant. "Wait. Would I have to walk down the aisle with Drew? Because nothing says 'lonely spinster' like having your brother as an escort."

"You would only walk with him at the end," Luke said, then smirked. "Unless you want me to ask Isaac Jones to be my best man?"

Hannah's response was to pick up a plump strawberry from the fruit salad and throw it at his head.

"Is someone going to fill me in on whatever is going on between you and Isaac?" Carmen asked.

Luke shook his head at his fiancée. "Don't ask or she might tell you."

"Do you know what he had the gall to do earlier today?" Hannah continued as though she hadn't heard them. "He tried to squeeze into a picture I was taking of Sammy."

Her brother used his finger to wipe off the red juice dribbling down his cheek. "Where was this picture being taken?"

"Inside the fire truck." Hannah looked down at one of her jagged thumbnails. Not that she was the type of woman who had time for manicures, but she also wasn't normally a nail biter. Or, at least, she hadn't been one in years. Just two sightings of Isaac and less than forty-eight hours later, her nails were bitten to the quick.

"Technically..." Carmen handed Luke a damp paper towel to wipe his face "...I believe it's called a fire engine."

"What did he do when you asked him to turn the taxpayers' fire *engine*—" Luke winked at his fiancée "—into your personal portrait studio?"

Hannah rolled her eyes. "It wasn't like I asked for special treatment or anything. In fact, if it'd been up to me, I would've kept as far away from him as possible. But you should've seen how Sammy's eyes lit up when he put on that helmet. My son is obviously way more important to me than a meaningless grudge some arrogant firefighter still hasn't gotten over ten years later."

"Hello?" Carmen's hand shot up into the air and she waved her fingers. "I'm still lost over here. What grudge? What's going on between you and Isaac?"

"Nothing!" Hannah wailed, then she lowered her voice when she spotted the kids playing outside the window. "Nothing is going on between us and it never will again."

"Again?"

"We dated briefly when we were teenagers." Actually, they'd done a lot more than date, but Hannah wasn't going to further humiliate herself by admitting to her brother and his fiancée how much more. Ten years ago, Hannah had been much more innocent—in more ways than one—and had thought Isaac was "the one." Currently, though, both pride and hindsight forced her to downplay how foolish she'd once been. "It really wasn't that big of a deal."

"As you can see," Luke grabbed for another slice of pepperoni, not even bothering to conceal his sneakiness this time. "Hannah's totally over him. She's only mentioned him about thirty-eight times since she got here tonight."

"No I haven't." Hannah crossed her arms in front of her chest. "I didn't even say a word about the video."

"What video?" Carmen asked and Hannah's jaw snapped shut.

"Somebody posted a breakup video on YouTube ten years ago," Luke explained, as though it was perfectly normal to end a relationship in an online rant to the entire world. Then he looked at Hannah. "Did you ever find out who did it?"

But she kept her lips locked in place. Why hadn't it ever occurred to her that Isaac wasn't necessarily responsible for posting it? And did it even matter? All that mattered was that he'd said the words.

"What do you mean, a breakup video?" Carmen asked.

When it became apparent that Hannah wasn't going to speak, Luke continued. "I forget the exact words he used, but it went something like, 'Hannah Gregson was done with me so she moved on to the next guy.'"

Actually, it was *Hannah Gregson is the ultimate user. She plays all innocent until she gets what she wants and moves on to the next guy. Well, guess what, Gregson? It's over and you'll never see me in Sugar Falls again. Too bad you just lost out on the* best *guy you'll get.* Not that Hannah had replayed it in her mind a thousand times.

"Ouch." Carmen frowned, not even knowing the worst part. Isaac's unpleasant speech had come right after they'd spent the night together. "How old was he when he did this?"

"Eighteen," Luke replied. "And, in his defense, his eyes were pretty watery at the time, as though he'd been drowning his sorrow in a case of cheap beer."

"In his defense?" Hannah finally spoke up. A bit too loudly. "You're supposed to be my brother, you know? Whatever happened to having each other's back?"

"You want me drive over to the fire station and beat him up for you?" he asked, and Hannah tilted her head as she pondered his offer. "Geez, I was kidding, Hannah. Even if I wanted to, I couldn't."

"Because of your job?" She nibbled at the cuticle on her thumb. Her brother was a former SEAL who was now the officer in charge of Navy recruitment for the entire region.

"No, because of his." Luke let out a deep breath when Hannah shot him a look of confusion. "Here's the deal. I know this might surprise you, but your precious nephews got into a little trouble at the Fourth of July picnic."

"Those angels?" Hannah looked out the window to where Aiden was tying each side of a kite to Caden's shoulders as they directed Sammy to run a tape measure from the top of a ladder to an oak tree in the middle of the yard. Carmen groaned before dashing outside to get them.

"I know. It's hard to believe." Luke chuckled. "I won't bore you with the details, but it involved a bag of hot dog buns, some firecrackers and Mayor Johnston's hand-carved cornhole set. Anyway, Isaac was on duty nearby and had the blaze put out before it did any real damage.

But he also gave the boys a solid lecture about fire safety and made them honorary junior deputies. Since then, they haven't so much as blown out a candle, let alone gotten anywhere near an open flame. So I kinda owe the guy."

"Well, I don't owe him a damn thing," Hannah replied.

She'd already given Isaac Jones way too much of herself.

By seven o'clock on Monday morning, most of the weekend tourists had left town and Sugar Falls was already bustling with locals returning to work. Isaac had just gotten off duty and decided to stop at Duncan's to pick up some groceries before heading back to his uncle's house.

Walking across the street from the fire station to the only market in town, he used his cell phone to call Jonesy, who answered on the first ring.

"Do we have any eggs?" Isaac asked.

"Not sure," the old man replied.

Isaac really needed to move into his own place and stock his own fridge. "What about milk?"

"Might have a little left."

A horn honked from somewhere down the street and Isaac heard the echo of the same honk on the speaker. "Where are you?"

"On my way to the Cowgirl Up Café to meet Scooter for breakfast," Jonesy said in a slow drawl.

Looking over his shoulder, he spotted his uncle a few hundred feet away, riding his horse in the middle of the road, a line of cars gridlocked behind them. Pinching the bridge of his nose, Isaac disconnected the phone and counted patiently until Jonesy cantered up to him. "I thought Mayor Johnston told you not to ride Klondike on the street anymore."

"He did. But then the folks over at city hall threw a walleyed fit when I started riding her on the sidewalk. So unless they're gonna put a horse trail through downtown, me and Klondike are gonna take advantage of any road my tax dollars pay for."

"You could drive your truck, you know."

"Then Klondike would miss out on those big, juicy apples Freckles gives her over at the café." His uncle patted the horse's spotted gray neck. "You like your treats, don'tcha, girl?"

"Well, maybe you should at least ride her in the bicycle lane," Isaac suggested.

"That's for bikes. You wanna grab some breakfast with me and Scooter?"

Isaac studied the older man, looked at the parking lot of the market then glanced at his watch. As a kid, the highlights of his summer used to be when he'd get to spend time with Jonesy and Scooter, his uncle's best friend, and listen to their countless stories. The two irreverent coots were staples in downtown Sugar Falls and loved to sit around talking about their days on the professional bull riding circuit, the action they saw in Vietnam and the latest prospects for the Boise State offensive line. They were both part of the volunteer fire department and mountain rescue team, but mostly they hung out gossiping about the locals and imparting unsolicited advice to anyone in their vicinity, peppering their conversations with the occasional conspiracy theory.

Isaac patted his empty stomach. He'd been out of town for a couple of weeks and hadn't had Freckles' country gravy in a while. Plus, it would be a good chance to catch up on the latest news. And by news, he meant information about Hannah Gregson and her sudden reentry into his life. "I guess I could go for some chicken-fried steak.

But I'll walk. And I'm a government employee, so if Mayor Johnston or Cessy Walker see you on that horse, I'm gonna *keep* on walking."

The Cowgirl Up Café was only two blocks down Snowflake Boulevard, the main street that ran through the center of the Victorian-era downtown. Although he lived in Jonesy's old cabin on Sugar Creek, Isaac spent most of his time at the new fire station, working out the kinks of turning a rural volunteer unit into a professional and efficiently run department. Proving to everyone that he would be the best fire chief this town had ever seen.

His mom had always pushed him to be the best at whatever he did. If it were up to his old man—Jonesy's brother—Isaac would've been handed everything on a silver platter. Hank—now Henry—Jones left Sugar Falls the day he turned eighteen and never looked back. He'd made his fortune in the stock market and vowed that no relative of his would ever have to worry about money again.

It was probably the biggest thing that his parents fought about, when they bothered to spend any time together. His mother was a young intern when she'd met and married his father and Henry never quite got over the fact that his supposed trophy wife ended up out-earning him by their third year of marriage. Neither one had wanted children, but Henry had talked her into just one child in the hopes that it would slow his wife's career path and turn her into a carpooling soccer mom.

Yet having Isaac only drove Rachel Jones to do better, to put in extra hours at the office, to make even more money. He was the wedge that had finally driven his parents apart. At least, that's how he'd always felt.

If Henry would buy their son the latest gaming console, Rachel would send him outside to work with the gardener in order to "earn" time to play video games. When Henry had taken Isaac aboard his private yacht for two months on the Mediterranean, Rachel decided to send her biracial son to spend his summers with a cranky, older uncle in a simple cabin on a mountain in Idaho—about as far from their Upper East Side lifestyle as she could get him. She'd thought it'd be the perfect way to not only get back at Henry, but also make Isaac appreciate the finer things that money could buy, which would make him want to become an even greater success than his parents.

His mom's goal of pushing Isaac to always rise above had worked and made him competitive at life. Just not at the career that she'd envisioned and thoroughly mapped out for him.

Because they were short-staffed until the latest batch of recruits graduated from the fire academy in Boise, Isaac had spent the past two days working double overnight shifts to cover for one of his deputy firefighters. He hadn't seen his uncle since the pancake breakfast on Saturday. While Isaac had been relieved to avoid Jonesy's nosy questions about the return of his ex-girlfriend, he also hadn't been able to gather any useful information.

When they walked through the saloon-style front doors of the restaurant, Isaac had to blink a few times to accustom himself to the bright purple and turquoise-blue decor. He'd been coming to the café since the summer after sixth grade, and the eclectic decorating style was no clearer to him now than it had been back then— he could never figure out if it looked more like a rustic bunkhouse on a ranch or a sequin-covered sorority house.

"Darlin'!" yelled Freckles, the owner and interior decorator. At least, he assumed she was the one responsible for the look of the place—judging from her brightly dyed orange hair, red cowboy boots, skintight leopard-print leggings and low-cut lime-green T-shirt that boasted We'll Butter Your Biscuit. "When'd you get back from your trainin'?"

"Late Friday night."

"Well then, I don't blame you for not stopping in and seeing me yet." Freckles carried a pot of coffee to the booth where Scooter was already sitting. "Not even the start of ski season, and this place was already a madhouse last weekend. Your old uncle here almost got himself eighty-sixed for coming in on Saturday and announcing to all my paying customers that my pancakes came from a *box* mix."

"Who are *you* callin' old?" Jonesy mumbled, flipping over a hot-pink coffee mug. Isaac kicked his uncle under the table. Nobody knew Freckles' exact age, and although it would probably be safe to estimate that the woman was nearing her eighth decade, it definitely wouldn't be prudent to mention it out loud.

"I'm putting you and Scooter on decaf." Freckles squinted, her long false eyelashes sticking together as she frowned at Jonesy. "I'm not dealing with any extra sass outta you two this mornin'."

Isaac chuckled, but his humorous mood was quickly cut short when the front door opened and Sammy appeared, wearing stiff jeans with creases and a brand new pair of sneakers. Hannah was right behind him, dressed in a long, bohemian-style skirt and a high-necked tank top, the arms of her denim jacket cinched around her waist.

For the second time today, he pinched the bridge of his nose. Isaac believed in a life lived with plenty of forgiveness and no regrets. But that had been before Hannah Gregson came crashing back into his universe with her cute kid. It was much easier to forgive a past grievance when he wasn't running into the person who'd done him wrong everywhere he went in this small town.

The top of her long, blond hair was loosely clipped, allowing the bottom locks to stream down her back in soft waves. The last two times he'd seen her, she'd had it pulled up. In fact, when they'd been teenagers, the only time he'd ever seen it completely down had been the night they'd sneaked off to the boatshed behind her family's cabin and she'd been peeling off her swimsuit with the lantern light glowing off her tanned skin...

He took a gulp of water, tilting the glass back so quickly that an ice cube slipped down his throat, causing him to sputter. Unfortunately, his cough caused everyone in the restaurant to look his way, including Sammy, whose face lit up with a crooked smile as he darted over.

"Hi, Chief Jones! Do you still have the photo of me on your phone?" The boy's accent seemed to deepen slightly with his excitement. "My mama said she forgot to ask you for a copy."

Forgot? After telling Isaac to get out of the picture, the woman had been so quick to rush off with her kid, she'd tossed his cell on the passenger seat of the fire engine and hadn't even said so much as a thank-you.

He took a pen out of his front T-shirt pocket and scribbled on his paper napkin. "This is my number. Tell your mom to text me and I'll send it to her."

Isaac told himself that it wasn't as if he wanted Hannah to have any more contact with him than necessary. He merely wanted her to acknowledge that he'd done something nice for her.

"I'll tell her." Sammy nodded. "Are you going to bring the fire engine to school today?"

"I hope not." Disappointment flashed across the kid's

face and Isaac amended, "But only because that would mean we were responding to a fire and nobody wants one of those disrupting how much fun you'll be having in your new class."

Sammy didn't seem quite convinced and Isaac sympathized with being the new kid in a different world. So he offered Sammy the same distraction Uncle Jonesy had once offered him when he'd been a child. "If you want to see the fire engine again, just come by the station anytime, big guy."

Hannah was at the counter, balancing two white bakery boxes in her arms but keeping a guarded eye on Sammy. While he doubted she could hear him, Isaac's stomach clenched at the realization that the woman probably wasn't a fan of him talking to her son, let alone giving out an open invitation to hang out at the fire station. Was she seriously that worried that he might be a bad influence? Or maybe she feared that Isaac would tell the kid about their shared past.

"Sweetie," Hannah called out to the child. "Can you come help me carry these to the car?"

The boy did an about-face and his new sneakers squeaked as he walked over to his mom. She stroked his head before giving his shoulder a reassuring squeeze. Isaac recalled his own first day at his elite boarding school in Connecticut. There hadn't been any affectionate affirmations or even parting words of wisdom. His father had a "business meeting" on the golf course and his mother was closing a deal in Taiwan. But her assistant had left an itemized packing list with the maid and a map with specific drop off instructions for their driver.

Sammy gave her a toothless grin and a thumbs up before carefully taking one of the containers.

"You're gonna need another set of hands to get these all out to your car, darlin'," Freckles admonished.

"We can make two trips." Hannah smiled at the waitress, but even from halfway across the restaurant, Isaac could see the pink flush stealing up her sucked-in cheeks and the steady way she avoided making eye contact with anyone.

He flashed back to the summer when they were seventeen. The baseball game she'd organized to raise money for a new bingo cage at the senior center got rained out before game time, and she'd been sitting, drenched, in the uncovered dugout. Isaac had pulled up in Jonesy's old truck and offered to drive her home. She'd confided in him how weak it made her feel when people thought she needed help—especially when she was the one who was supposed to be helping others. She'd admitted that she'd always been the baby of her family and with her twin brothers' recent enlistment in the Navy, she was finally getting the freedom to spread her wings and prove that she could be just as strong and as capable as them. Unfortunately, in her determination to make the world a better place, she also hadn't had the foresight to get her driver's license before deciding to tackle all of her charitable goals.

If he had to pinpoint the start of their relationship, it would be that day, when the sweet and beautiful girl who claimed she didn't need anybody finally accepted his help. It had all been downhill after that.

Jonesy kicked him under the table and used his whiskered chin to nod toward Hannah.

What? he mouthed at Jonesy.

"He wants you to go help her, son!" Scooter's booming voice drew everyone's attention. The last thing Isaac wanted was to have the townspeople speculating about the new fire chief, the returning teacher and their disastrous past together. Not that they weren't already doing exactly that.

"No need," Hannah said, turning toward the exit so quickly that her hair swirled in waves down her back. "I'll come back for the rest."

The only way to stop the stares—and the speculation—was to get Hannah out of the restaurant as soon as possible.

Chapter Four

Isaac stood quickly and was at the counter in five strides. He picked up the remaining three bakery boxes and followed Sammy, who was trailing his mother out of the café.

The smell of sugar and cinnamon made his head dizzy as he watched her retreating rear end cross the sidewalk to where several cars—and two horses—were parked at the curb, her flowing skirt swishing with each of her hurried steps.

Isaac recalled the summer he was fifteen, when Hannah had worn a Save Our Planet T-shirt and organized a recycling drive at the park square in the center of town. He would've expected her to be driving some low-emission hybrid automobile and not the behemoth of a gas-guzzling jalopy she was currently unlocking.

"Is this really your car?" he asked, then cringed as

she dropped one of the containers she'd been balancing in her free arm.

She groaned, then turned to face him. "No, it's not. And what are you doing here?"

"I'm helping you carry…" he looked down at his boxes "…whatever this is."

"They're cinnamon rolls. It's Nurse Dunn's birthday today and normally the principal would bring in breakfast treats to celebrate with the other teachers. But Dr. Cromartie was taken to the hospital with appendicitis over the weekend, so I volunteered to pick them up."

Of course she did, Isaac thought. But before he could comment on her constant need for martyrdom, she lowered her voice and added, "I *meant*, what are you doing in Sugar Falls?"

He took a step back at her accusatory tone. "I live here."

"But why?"

"I'm guessing for the same reason you want to live here. Because I like it."

"I thought you liked the East Coast better. You were certainly eager enough to go back there. Couldn't you have gotten a job with the Yale Fire Department or something?"

"First of all, no. Yale is a college, not a city, so they don't technically have their own fire department."

She huffed before bending down to pick up the cinnamon rolls she'd dropped. "I was being facetious."

Hannah took the box from Sammy, whose wide eyes were bouncing back and forth between the two adults arguing on the sidewalk. She pulled one of the fresh baked treats out and passed it to him. "Everything is fine, sweetie. Grab a napkin out of the glove box in case you get icing on your shirt and then buckle up."

As the boy climbed inside, she turned back to Isaac. Her full pink lips parted, but before she could resume her attack, Isaac said, "Second of all, Sugar Falls needed a chief for the new fire department and I was the most qualified candidate for the position."

"They must not have had a very big pool of applicants." Hannah used her key to open the trunk, then snatched the top two boxes from the stack in his arms—a bit forcefully, in his opinion. However, he wasn't going to take the bait. He stepped around her to set the rest of the cinnamon rolls in the car, but she didn't get out of his way in time, causing his biceps to brush against the soft cotton covering her breast.

It felt as if someone had lit a match inside his chest and his skin tightened as she gasped.

"Third of all..." He schooled his features so she wouldn't be able to see that the accidental contact had affected him as much as it had her. "I have just as much right to live here as you do."

"But I lived here first." She slammed the car door and put her hands on her hips, which only served to draw his gaze to her full breasts.

"You didn't live here six months ago when I took the position. Trust me. I checked."

She narrowed her eyes. "You checked on where I was living?"

"Apparently not well enough." The truth was that he hadn't asked his uncle directly because Isaac didn't want Jonesy to think he'd never gotten over her. But he'd tried to bring it up in casual conversation with Scooter Deets, who obviously wasn't a reliable source. All he'd told Isaac was that the last he'd heard, Hannah was living somewhere overseas doing charity work. "So it looks like you're stuck with me now."

"Unlike some people, I don't live in the past, Isaac. I'm all about forgiveness and moving on."

He gave an awkward half snort. "Yeah, ten years ago you certainly moved on from me quickly enough—with Carter Mahoney, as I recall."

In his line of work, Isaac knew that the hottest fires came from a combination of oxygen and gas to create pinpoint blue flames. Hannah's eyes had just flared into that exact shade as she replied, "And now I'm suddenly remembering why that was such a smart decision."

She pivoted, marching haughtily around the car and got in. Sammy waved at him from the backseat as Hannah gunned the engine and drove off, not having the decency to look back herself and see how deeply her words had cut him.

The end of October couldn't come soon enough for Hannah. Nor could the end of the trick-or-treat jog-a-thon she'd been way too eager to organize only a few days after her return. Hannah was still learning how to balance a full-time job with being a full-time single parent. Several months ago, when she'd told her parents that she was going through the steps to adopt Sammy, they'd shrieked with joy. They'd even devised a schedule to spend more time in Sugar Falls to help with childcare and get to know their new grandson.

But that had all been before her mom's breast cancer recurrence.

Hannah should've known better than to add more activities to her already growing responsibilities. However, keeping her mind occupied left less opportunity to think about all the things she was trying to push to the back of her brain.

Unfortunately, no matter how busy Hannah had kept

this week, she remained unsuccessful in her attempts to avoid Isaac around town. It probably didn't help that she wasn't much of a cook and tended to buy prepared meals on the run, making it easier for her son—who had an uncanny knack for spotting the firefighter in any crowd—to pepper Isaac with dozens of questions.

She'd already run into him at Duncan's Market—literally. Cringing, she remembered everyone staring as she crashed her cart into his near the ready-made rotisserie chicken display before mumbling an apology and hiding out in the cereal aisle, not coming near the checkstand until she heard his walkie-talkie crackle to life and saw him jog out of the store. Two nights later, when she and Sammy were sick of eating corn flakes for dinner because she'd forgotten to go back and get the chicken, Isaac held the door open for her at Domino's Deli and then proceeded to stand there for ten minutes listening to her son tell him all about his favorite sandwich toppings.

No matter where she went, she constantly ran the risk of seeing him. Or seeing someone who wanted to talk about him. Like Elaine Marconi, the president of the PTA who had gone behind Hannah's back and invited the Sugar Falls police and fire departments to participate in today's fundraiser. The woman had claimed having the local heroes would help motivate and inspire the students who were grumbling about having to run.

Now Hannah was the only one grumbling. She tried not to watch Isaac and one of his crews, along with Carmen and several off-duty officers, as they raced along the elementary-school track, giving kids high fives and leading them in singing military-themed cadences. It was like she couldn't get away from the man.

A few days ago, when Luke had pointed out that Isaac might have been crying during the video ten years ago, or at least been intoxicated, Hannah had experienced a brief softening in her heart. Extremely brief. The following morning, Sammy had run over to him at the Cowgirl Up Café as though he was a long lost family friend and Hannah had reacted the only way she knew how—by trying to shield her son from the inevitable hurt the man was sure to bring.

Then, after he'd insisted on helping her carry the cinnamon rolls to her brother's car, he'd made that snide remark about the only person who'd supported her that awful summer. Carter Mahoney had been the one to take her aboard his father's boat and shuttle her back to the marina after Elaine had told her what Isaac really thought of her. Carter'd been the one to sit in the cab of his truck with her when she'd cried those heavy tears of shame and betrayal, too hurt and shocked to talk about it and too embarrassed to go home and face her parents. And Carter had been the one who'd driven over to her cabin, his laptop under one arm as he gently broke the news to her about the break-up video.

"Sammy sure does love to run," Nurse Dunn said from under the canopy where they'd set up the first-aid station. Needing a distraction from all these unwelcome memories, Hannah could either stand here and make small talk with the middle-aged school nurse or she could hide in the huddle of other parents who were passing out drinks at the refreshment table.

Hannah had inadvertently taken the reins on this event and it was her responsibility to see it through. Besides, if the kids could stand the sun and the unseasonable heat while wearing their Halloween costumes, then so could she. At least on this side of the field, Nurse Dunn seemed more interested in talking about Hannah's son than about her ex-boyfriend. Elaine Marconi and several other moms gathered near the bleachers on the opposite side of the field wouldn't give her the same consideration.

"He does," Hannah agreed, pride blossoming in her chest at her child's steady pace and happy smile as he dashed past some fourth graders. "No matter where we go, he'd rather run than walk. I can hardly keep up with him sometimes."

"I've always thought about doing foster care or adopting," the nurse commented with a hint of speculation in her voice. Hannah held her breath, waiting for all the personal questions that would surely come next. But the woman simply said, "Now that my own kids are out of the house, I might look into it."

Hannah released the air in her lungs, relieved that Nurse Dunn seemed to understand the need for due diligence and research when starting the adoption process, instead of leaping without looking. She'd be glad to talk to anyone who had a sincere interest and wasn't just digging for details about Sammy's background. In fact, she was about to offer more information on the subject, but a first grader with Princess Leia buns limped toward the first-aid station and the school nurse sprang into action. Hannah was so distracted by the little girl's arrival that she didn't notice Isaac's approach.

"Everything okay over here?" His voice came from behind her and Hannah fumbled the clipboard in her hand. That was the second time he'd startled her to the point of making her drop something. She clenched her teeth together as she bent down to retrieve it.

"Just a little blister," Nurse Dunn replied. "After twenty-eight years on the job, I could bandage these things in my sleep."

Rising, Hannah's gaze traveled up the defined lines of

Isaac's toned, bare legs, past his blue running shorts and stopped when it got to his snug fire department tee. Her face heated at the memory of him jogging most summer mornings without a shirt, and Hannah was both thankful and slightly disappointed that they were at a school-sponsored function today and he was properly clothed. While he'd been lean and muscular back then, she could tell through the damp cotton covering his torso that he'd bulked up since high school and his body was even more impressive now.

Her mouth went dry and she tried to remind herself that good looks were just one more thing that came easy to Isaac. He'd always excelled at everything. Except getting her.

He'd actually had to put some effort into that, spending the entire summer after eleventh grade showing up wherever Hannah was, offering her rides and friendship and a connection that she hadn't been able to form with anyone else in Sugar Falls. They'd emailed each other during their senior year of school, and the next June, when they both returned to Sugar Falls, they'd been inseparable. Right up to that night in the boatshed when she'd freely given him her virginity.

Then, the very next day, he'd gone back to being the rich guy with the ski boat, not even picking her up for the Labor Day bonfire because he was too busy teaching several girls how to wakeboard.

"I think I'm going to see if they need more water at the refreshment station," Hannah mumbled as she commanded her feet to move, trying to get far away from Isaac. Far away from his sexy, deep voice that still sent blasts of heat all the way down to her toes.

Whoa. She really could use a cold drink right about now to cool her down. Unfortunately, as she approached the other pop-up tent near the bleachers, she overheard someone else talking about adoption, and this time it wasn't as well-meaning as Nurse Dunn's comment.

"I just don't see why she had to get one from a whole other country. I mean, aren't there enough kids here in America that need good homes…?" Elaine Marconi's hushed voice trailed off when another mom—who must've spotted Hannah before anyone else—loudly cleared her throat.

Hannah bristled and she opened her mouth to tell Elaine exactly what she should do with her opinions. But Marcia Duncan, the owner of Duncan's Market, added more fuel to the proverbial fire by letting out a whistle. "Woo-hoo. Check out Chief Jones on the track. Have you ever seen such a fine specimen of man before?"

Several other women hummed in agreement and one bold lady even offered a "Yowza."

If Hannah's skin was bristling before, it was now in full porcupine mode. But Elaine and Marcia were blatantly focused on her, both with their eyes rounded and locked in on their latest target. They were clearly hoping for a reaction and Hannah would be damned if she provided these busybodies with any more ammunition.

"I heard that Isaac comes with two separate trust funds. One from his mom and one from his daddy," Marcia continued. "The man's got to be as rich as sin, but he lives in Jonesy's rundown log house out by Sugar Creek and spends his days at that fire station doing a blue collar job when he probably never has to work a day in his life."

Hannah reached for one of the Gatorades that had been set out for the runners and downed it before squeezing the empty paper cup in her fist. She felt Elaine's eyes studying her, looking for the slightest sign of weakness. The woman thrived on drama, and Hannah braced herself for the next snarky comment. They hadn't gotten along when they were teenagers and they certainly hadn't been on the best of terms since Hannah had placed Elaine's son Jake in a lower level reading group two years ago.

"Makes you wonder why a man like that would be so determined to stay in a place like this. Unless he's only thinking with his…you-know-what." Elaine's zinger was delivered with as much subtlety as a thresher shark stunning its prey and Hannah didn't have to look down to where the woman was pointing to get Elaine's crude reference. "Although, from what I remember about Isaac Jones, he never had to work too hard when it came to women."

That's it. Hannah grabbed another Gatorade and turned to head back to the nurse's tent. Unfortunately, she pivoted too abruptly and the red liquid in her cup splashed straight onto Isaac's sweaty T-shirt.

One minute he was making another lap around the field, the next Isaac felt sticky rivulets of red sports drink run down his chest. But that was secondary to the tightness he felt inside his ribcage at the obvious distress written all over Hannah's face.

Surely she wasn't embarrassed by an accidental spill? She held her lips in a rigid line and barely opened them as she stiffly grounded out the words, "Sorry about that."

It was then that he noticed about half a dozen women clustered behind Hannah, their gazes clearly riveted on the scene unfolding before them. He recognized several of them from their teenage days and it suddenly dawned on him that Hannah's obvious tension might have nothing to do with him at all.

"Don't worry about it," he said quickly, wanting to relieve her discomfort despite not knowing what the cause was. He reached behind his neck and grabbed the back of his collar before yanking the wet cotton fabric over his head. "I've got several more T-shirts just like this one in my truck."

Several gasps and possibly a whistle came from the onlooking women and Hannah's hand immediately shot out and pried the tee from his hand. The damp and now cold stickiness was pressed back onto his chest as she shoved the tee at him and hissed under her breath, "Put it back on. You're only making things worse."

"Making what worse?" Isaac asked. Hannah's head gave a very subtle jerk toward the murmuring moms behind her who weren't even pretending not to witness whatever was going on between Hannah and Isaac at that exact second. However, he didn't care about their reaction when all he could focus on was the way Hannah's pupils dilated as her gaze dropped to his bare shoulders. A tingling of awareness pumped through him as her eyes flickered lower and he tightened his ab muscles in response.

Just then, Sammy jogged up to them, the hem of his Batman T-shirt already lifted up to expose his own little-kid belly above a yellow plastic utility belt. "Hey, Chief, if you're not going to wear your fireman shirt, can I wear it? Mama took me to three different stores to find a fireman costume, but they only had superhero ones left."

"No, sweetie." Hannah squatted down. With the whispers and giggles growing in the background, he could barely hear her quiet words to her son. "Chief Isaac just spilled something on himself. But he's going to put his shirt back on right now because there's a dress code at school and *everybody* has to wear their clothes."

She pointed the last comment in his direction and Isaac groaned as he pulled the sticky—and now tangled—shirt over his head so he wouldn't set a bad example.

"Come on, Sammy," Hannah said, casting an annoyed glance over her shoulder at two of Sugar Falls' biggest gossips. "I'll run the last lap with you."

Hannah's slip-ons flapped against her heels as she began jogging next to the excited boy and she kicked the shoes off onto the grassy field. Watching her run barefoot on the dirt track, Isaac's chest filled with pride. He'd always respected the way Hannah stood up for her beliefs and he wouldn't have been surprised if she'd called the snickering women to task. He respected her even more for showing the grace and forethought to teach her child how to finish strong, even in the face of bad manners.

Running to catch up with Sammy, Isaac called out, "Wait for me."

Yet, as he increased his speed, Hannah increased hers, keeping a few paces ahead of him. He could see the slight pivot of her head as she kept looking behind her, her ponytail whipping back and forth.

"You're not going to outrun me, Hannah," he told her when he easily lengthened his strides. "Or is it something else you're trying to escape?"

"You know I'm not a runner," she replied, her breath coming in shorter pants. "In all senses of the word."

"She really isn't," Sammy said, oblivious to his mother's double meaning. The boy slowed his pace and took Hannah's hand, tugging her along. "I always beat her when we race."

"And what do you get when you beat her?" Isaac asked the boy.

"I get a hug and sometimes an extra scoop of ice cream at dinner." Sammy smiled proudly, revealing his two missing teeth.

"Then I'll wait for my hug at the finish line," Isaac said before launching into a full sprint.

Sammy got there next and launched himself into Isaac's arms. Hannah's hug, however, was less enthusiastic when she finally arrived, her cheeks flushed and her chest heaving between gulps of air. She tried to do one of those one-armed side hugs, but Isaac rotated at the last minute and pulled her right up against his wet, sticky T-shirt.

She gasped, but her arms wrapped around his neck, probably because he'd swept her off her bare feet. Sammy giggled and clapped his hands in approval, which only encouraged Isaac to hold on to her longer. Hannah felt so good pressed against him, his voice was low and hoarse when he set her back down and whispered in her ear. "I'll be looking forward to that ice cream, too."

Chapter Five

"How about a rummage sale?" one of the townspeople in the audience called from his seat. "The middle school raised over four hundred dollars when we held one last spring."

Hannah had to stifle a yawn. It wasn't the worst idea put forth at the council meeting, but it definitely wasn't going to rake in the bucks, either. Didn't these people know how to generate excitement? Geez.

Mayor Johnston's microphone buzzed the way it always did when he put his bushy, gray mustache up against it to speak. "The city is gonna need to bring in a lot more money than that for this year's Ski Potato Festival and Parade."

The members of the city council nodded in agreement with their leader, but so far, none of the fifty or so people in attendance at the November meeting had provided any reasonable suggestions. Hannah tapped the toe of her ankle boot, waiting for everybody else's fundraising ideas to get shot down before she presented hers.

Every year since incorporating in 1906, the town of Sugar Falls hosted the Ski Potato Festival during the winter holiday season. What had started out as a small, local tradition had blossomed into a bustling tourist attraction for all the out-of-towners who liked partaking of the mountain's lush pine forests and early snowfall. Before Hannah left for Ghana, the festival had already been one of the biggest local events, and while it brought in a hefty amount of tourist dollars, it also required some financial help to put on.

Three years ago, Hannah had headed up the fundraising committee. However, in her absence, the volunteer efforts had unfortunately run into a few hiccups. It wasn't that Hannah didn't like Cessy Walker, the wealthy socialite who sat in the seat next to Mayor Johnston at the head table, or appreciate the older woman's efforts to want the best for their town.

It was just that Cessy sometimes forgot that most of the Sugar Falls locals weren't raking in the alimony checks like she was. Most of them weren't the type of people who could afford to vacation at Snow Creek Lodge, the luxurious ski resort up the road. Hannah's neighbors certainly couldn't spend a thousand dollars for a ticket to a themed Dinner with a Star event, despite the fact that Cessy Walker claimed she could get Barry Manilow as the guest of honor when she'd suggested the idea a few minutes ago.

Marcia Duncan's words last week about Isaac's wealth and his reasons for staying in Sugar Falls skipped through Hannah's mind and she squeezed her eyes closed to squelch them down. She wasn't at this meeting to think about her ex. Or the way he'd picked her up into a tight, sweaty hug after the Halloween run. She was here to represent her community.

Hannah's brother Luke, who was watching Sammy so that she could attend this evening, had warned Hannah not to come on too strong at her first city council meeting since her return. He possibly had a point, since she'd only been back in town for a couple weeks, but the jog-a-thon had been a financial success, and now Hannah was itching to put her fundraising skills to more use. While she might not be any good with dating or relationships, given her reaction to Isaac running that last lap with her and Sammy last week, she could more than hold her own when it came to charity events.

Luke, unfortunately, was too carefree to understand Hannah's restlessness, and he was too happy in his new life to understand her need to prove herself. *Ease back into things, sis*, he'd told her. *And whatever you do, don't start lecturing everyone about their civic and moral responsibilities.*

Whatever that was supposed to mean. Hannah shifted in her metal folding chair before crossing her legs, then uncrossing them for the hundredth time that night. It was all she could do to sit there quietly and listen. Glancing back at Carmen, who stood against the auditorium wall in her blue police uniform, Hannah decided that she'd waited long enough. But before she could politely raise her hand and offer up a more realistic suggestion, Freckles stood up in the front row.

The café owner was wearing faux leather pants—at least, Hannah hoped the material was fake because she couldn't imagine an animal's skin being that exact shade of red—and a purple sweatshirt with a clock and the words Half Past Wine O'Clock printed on the back. Freckles could command the attention of the entire room just by her clothing selection, yet she spoke in a laid-back, comfortable twang as though she was explaining the day's lunch specials. "I say we have one of those bachelor auctions."

Several murmurs immediately sounded from the audience and Hannah was sure none of them had heard the older lady correctly. Mayor Johnston's mustache scratched against the microphone. "Anyone want to second that?"

Hannah lowered her forehead into her palms and massaged her temples as the auditorium broke into chaos, a third of the people present speaking at once.

"I think a bachelor auction would be a fantastic idea." Cessy Walker leaned in front of the mayor and spoke into his microphone. "And it's something we've never done before here in Sugar Falls."

A twitch developed in the corner of Hannah's eyelid, causing a series of rapid-fire blinks. She wanted to scream that they've never done it because it was a horrible idea. It was demeaning for the bachelors and she could hardly imagine any of the women in town actually being desperate enough to bid on them. It was tacky and ostentatious. Besides, it would be a tremendous failure. If she didn't slam the brakes on this plan right now, they would be here all night.

"You guys," Hannah said as she stood up. Then she had to clear her throat and raise her voice to be heard above the excited voices.

"You guys!" she repeated, using her loudest teacher tone, which successfully quieted most of the talkers. She waited until she had everyone's attention before she began to speak. "We cannot put on a bachelor auction."

"Sounds like a great idea to me," Mayor Johnston replied then looked in Freckles' direction. "In fact, I'll be your first volunteer."

"The hell you will," the mayor's wife, who was sitting behind Hannah, said without bothering to look up from her smartphone. The woman had a well-known addiction to Candy Crush and an even better-known rein on her husband.

"See?" Hannah tried to smile at the mayor. "We don't even have eligible bachelors to bid on."

"Of course we do." Cessy Walker yanked the microphone in front of herself. "In fact, I see at least three of them in this room alone, not counting Scooter and Jonesy."

"Hey, now," Scooter Deets yelled a bit too loudly as he adjusted his hearing aid. "Why don't me and Jonesy count? We're both as single as they come."

"Because nobody would bid on a date that involves riding on the back of a horse through downtown," Cessy replied, then pointed a long, manicured finger. "But they'd certainly bid on Ethan Renault over there. And both of them."

Hannah pivoted to see Isaac and Clausson standing against the back wall near Carmen. Collapsing into her chair, Hannah was grateful for the slippery, cold metal that allowed her to slide low enough to hide behind Mae Johnston's steel-gray curls. She'd successfully been avoiding him since that breath-stealing hug at the jog-a-thon last week, but her luck had only lasted so long. When had he slipped into the room? And how could Hannah slip out?

"Chief Jones," Mayor Johnston boomed into the mic. "You and some of your men would be willing to volunteer as our bachelors, right? Maybe any extra money we raise can go toward that new brush truck that didn't make this year's budget?"

A woman Hannah recognized from the human resources office at City Hall ran to the mayor's side and whispered something in the man's ear. Probably a warning about what kind of lawsuits could arise from pimping out some of his government employees, even if it was for a charitable cause.

Yet the question still hung in the air. Along with the rest of the audience, Hannah slowly turned her head to catch a peek at Isaac's response. A giggle bubbled up in her throat. If there was one bright spot to this unorganized and fruitless city council meeting, it was seeing Isaac's jaw lock and his eyes widen in alarm.

"I'm on duty that day," he replied, yet Hannah recognized the discomfort in his voice. It always went an octave lower when he was nervous. Or when they were in the dark and he was telling Hannah to...

"Don't be ridiculous, darlin'," Freckles called back to him. "We haven't even set a date yet. We can work around your schedule."

"So we've got Chief Jones and the new guy and Ethan." Cessy wrote on a note pad without looking up at the choking sound coming from Luke's former Navy SEAL buddy. "Carmen, see if any of your police officers want to challenge the firefighters to see who can get the highest bids."

"I'll make some phone calls around town and get us some more men," Freckles added, making Hannah wonder how long the two old friends had been plotting this idea together.

"Don't forget about us." Jonesy gestured at himself and Scooter. "Put our names down on your list."

"But hold off on putting down any names from my

department until I talk with my guys first," Isaac said, causing several disappointed sighs from women in the audience.

"Afraid my department will get more bids than yours?" Carmen finally spoke up and Hannah squeezed her eyes shut.

Great. The challenge had officially been issued and there was no way that Isaac would back down now. He always had to come out ahead.

The cheers and whistles returned, along with those old stirrings of jealousy that Hannah thought were long gone. It was like Elaine's comment the other day had reawakened all those teenage insecurities. While Hannah shouldn't care about the obvious fact that there were women out there who might want a date with Isaac, she also wasn't about to be subjected to watching the bidding. She jumped to her feet with a new suggestion.

"Instead of a bachelor auction, why don't we do a dinner dance at the VFW?" she offered. "We can have a band and keep a percentage of the drink sales. We'll probably make much more money and then everyone in town, *including all the married couples and happily single people*, can participate and feel like they're contributing."

Okay, so maybe she didn't need to emphasize the fact that she was more than content with her own relationship status. Yet it was important for them all to understand that there were more inclusive ways to raise money. Ways that didn't involve gossip and speculation about who was willing to spend money in order to go out with the sexy single men of Sugar Falls. Including her ex.

"That's a perfect idea." Cessy beamed at her, and Hannah finally felt some of the tension ease in the back of her neck. Until the socialite added, "We'll do the bachelor auction on a Friday night and have a dance at the

VFW on Saturday night. You guys can bring your dates to the dance."

It took every ounce of strength Hannah possessed not to lean forward and put her head between her knees to brace for impact.

"How do you not own a single tie?" Cessy Walker, the bachelor auction co-organizer and wealthy know-it-all, asked Isaac two weeks later as they stood backstage at the Remington.

The rumor mill about tonight's event had gotten a bit out of hand and, due to a larger than expected turnout, the organizers had to relocate everything to a larger venue. Now, the old theater in town was packed.

Isaac hadn't thought there were that many single women in Sugar Falls. But as he peeked out from behind the heavy maroon curtain and scanned the faces in the audience, he realized that most of the crowd was probably only there for the spectacle of the thing.

Maybe this bachelor auction wasn't such a good idea after all. He hated formal dances and he hated people throwing their money away when he wasn't exactly doing anything to earn it except stand there and look single.

Was it too late to back out?

The older woman yanking on his collar got his attention. "What did you say, Ms. Walker?"

"I mean, don't get me wrong," she continued, as if he should already know what she'd been talking about. "I'm glad you didn't borrow one of your uncle's old bolo ties, but you could've at least thrown on a sport coat or done something to spiff yourself up."

"I wasn't aware that I needed spiffing. You do know I'm not really selling anything, right?"

Cessy unrolled the cuffs of his oxford shirt before seeing how wrinkled they were and rolling the sleeves back up. "Do you want to beat those fresh-faced pups from the police station or not?"

Isaac grunted as his fingers fought Cessy Walker's pointy red nails for custody of the third button on his shirt. "I'm pretty sure the HR supervisor would frown upon government employees showing off all their chest hair to beg for donations."

"The HR supervisor just bought a date with your head paramedic for two hundred and forty dollars. Besides, the city attorney said you signed the voluntary consent form."

"Voluntary? Is that what you and your buddy Freckles call it?" Isaac gave a sideways look toward the red-headed waitress on stage, a microphone pressed to the old gal's lips. She barked out bachelor stats and prices a mile a minute, as though this wasn't the first time she'd performed auctioneer duties. "You two roped Carmen into your scheme to appeal to my competitive spirit. Everyone knows there's only two people in this town who can't say no to a challenge—especially one for charity."

"Well, at least one of you showed up." Cessy squinted at a spot behind Isaac's shoulder.

His antennae perked up. "What do you mean *one* of us?"

But before Isaac could figure out if the socialite's comment also referred to Hannah, Freckles announced his name and Cessy all but shoved him out onto the stage.

He recovered from the initial stumble, trying to make his way toward center stage to stand on the masking-tape X, just as the surprisingly strong Cessy had instructed earlier. The stage lights were blinding, which was actually somewhat of a relief because that meant he couldn't see the crowd in front of him.

But he could hear them over the strains of George

Strait singing about being called a fireman who put out old flames. As far as firefighter songs went, it could've been much worse. Still. If he ever got his hands on the DJ, there would be hell to pay.

Stage fright momentarily flooded Isaac's body, freezing his muscles—despite the fact that there were several squealing cheers, along with an appreciative wolf whistle coming from the audience.

Freckles appeared from the opposite side of the stage, standing close enough to rest her bony elbow on his shoulder, making him unable to keep his hands on his hips without looking even more off-balance than he already did.

She gave his biceps a not-so-reassuring squeeze before speaking into the mic. "Our next bachelor's bio can be found on page five of your catalog."

"There's a catalog?" Isaac's head whipped around. "And how did you get my bio?"

Freckles ignored him as she continued to sell her latest product like a smooth-talking snake-oil salesman. "Sugar Falls' very own fire chief is six feet one and a hundred and eighty-five pounds of heroic muscle. His hobbies include running up flights of stairs with hoses, cooking gourmet meals at the fire station, reading true crime stories and driving his speedboat on Rush Lake."

Most people didn't know about his reading habits, so Isaac scanned the first few rows for his Uncle Jonesy, the traitor, but had to squint his eyes against the glare. It was too dim to see into the back of the theater, but if Jonesy or Scooter were here, they would've been front and center, slapping their knees and guffawing with laughter.

Freckles continued with her colorful description that made Isaac sound like a royal prince—or a royal fake, depending on who was asked. And from the sounds of things, there were plenty of people present to ask. He wondered if Hannah was one of them. Or had she been too chicken to show?

He would've been relieved that she wasn't on hand to witness this whole farce if he wasn't so disappointed. He knew Hannah well enough to know that she didn't miss out on an opportunity to raise money or awareness for a good cause. Unless she was making some sort of statement. In this case, she was clearly using her absence to convey the message that she was completely over him and couldn't be bothered. Her indifference stung more than it should.

"Isaac." Freckles shoved the microphone into his face, making his head jerk back in surprise. "Tell the lucky ladies out there about the special date you have planned."

Oh, hell. This was really happening.

Not that he had any control over the event, but a small, unreasonable part of him hoped that he *would* get the highest bid of the night, just to show Hannah what she was missing.

Chapter Six

Taking in a deep breath, Isaac tried to remind himself that he was here for a good cause. Namely, a new brush truck for his department.

Unfortunately, Isaac had never been one for romantic gestures, and the idea of misleading a woman into thinking that they were on an actual date didn't sit well with him. Plus, public speaking wasn't exactly his top skill and he hated not doing something in his wheelhouse. He inhaled through his nostrils, then spoke into the microphone. "I'll, uh, pick my date up at, uh, a place of her choosing and escort her to the dinner dance at the VFW hall tomorrow evening."

"Simmer down there, Romeo." Freckles' lowered voice was heavy with sarcasm. "We're trying to upsell the date, not set a record for the worst bargain. Could you at least offer something more than the bare minimum?"

There were no cheers or shrieks of delight from the

audience like there had been when Clausson promised to take *his* date for predinner drinks and a sunset cruise aboard his sailboat on Lake Rush.

"We're gonna start the bidding at two hundred dollars," Freckles spoke into the microphone, and Isaac worried that his neck was at severe risk for long-term damage from all the whipping around his head was doing. Who in the world would pay that kind of money to go to a community dance at the VFW with him? He didn't even dance.

"Two hundred," a woman's voice called out from the back of the audience. Isaac couldn't see who it was, but he knew who it *wasn't*. Nope. He wasn't going to think about Hannah tonight. He rolled his shoulders back and forced a smile toward whoever had called out the first bid.

Hopefully the lady would get her money's worth and he wouldn't still be thinking of Hannah on this upcoming date.

Just when he thought the agony was finally over, another person yelled, "Two-fifty."

"I have two-fifty," Freckles announced. "Do I hear two seventy-five?"

The original bidder countered with three hundred dollars and that's when things took a turn for the worse. A third female joined in and more prices were called out as the bidding escalated between the women he couldn't even see. If it wasn't Hannah bidding, then it didn't matter who bought the date.

"We're up to five hundred dollars." Freckles' voice was a bit more high-pitched than it had been when she'd originally started, and her heavily lined eyes eagerly darted out into the audience as she scanned the crowd, as though she could see something he couldn't. "That's the highest bid of the night so far, folks."

"Isn't this the part where you're supposed to say going once, going twice?" Isaac said between clenched teeth. He no longer cared about how much money he was raising for the town, he just wanted to get this whole spectacle over and done with.

"Just wait for it," Freckles murmured out the side of her mouth as she lowered her microphone and studied the audience members, their voices rising in whispered speculation.

"Wait for *what*? You have to be kiddi—"

"Eight hundred dollars," a deep baritone voice called out, making the entire theater go quiet. Isaac squeezed his eyes shut and forgot about the live mic when he uttered a curse. Not because it was a male who had done the bidding. But because the man was Luke Gregson. Hannah's brother.

This time, Freckles quickly—and a bit too gleefully, if you asked Isaac—hollered out, "Sold!"

"I don't think it's fair to—" he began, but Freckles was shushing him and shoving him toward the wings of the stage. She was already introducing the next bachelor when Cessy Walker looped her arm through his and steered him past the velvet curtain.

"Ms. Walker," Isaac started again once he was backstage. "There has got to be some sort of rule about who gets to—"

"We already established that people can bid by proxy and all dates, once paid for, are transferable." Cessy gave him a dismissive wave, but Isaac wasn't comforted or even the least bit appeased.

Transferable? What did *that* mean?

Had Hannah sent her brother to bid on her behalf? He highly doubted it, but Isaac clearly wasn't going to get any answers standing back here and arguing about the auction rules. Instead, he dashed toward the side door exit and looped around to the cashier table in the theater lobby to confront Luke Gregson.

When the former Navy SEAL swaggered up with a cocky smile on his face, he didn't even look at Isaac. Instead he asked Elaine Marconi, who was acting as cashier, "Do you take credit cards?"

"Gregson," Isaac all but growled, then paused when the man turned a smug grin in his direction. Unable to share in—or even understand—Luke's apparent satisfaction, Isaac narrowed his eyes and continued. "I'm assuming you didn't spend eight hundred dollars so that *you* could go with me to the VFW dance."

"Safe assumption."

"So…" Isaac prompted as Elaine scanned Luke's credit card through a tiny machine. But Elaine was also eagerly looking between the two men as though she was she was dying of thirst and they were fighting over a bucket of water.

"So, I'm getting married in two weeks," Luke said matter-of-factly.

"I know. I sent my RSVP card in the mail."

"And my sister will obviously be at the wedding."

Isaac managed a terse nod. It wasn't like he could pretend that he hadn't thought about that exact thing when he'd gotten the invite. But he worked in the same public safety building as Carmen and their departments were small enough that they often got called out to the same scenes to work together. Everyone else at his station would be attending, and it would raise too many questions if he didn't go.

He'd gone back and forth over his decision, knowing that he couldn't win either way. Stay away and cause speculation, or go and cause more tension between himself and Hannah. Yet the truth was that he wanted to see her. He wanted to clear the air. He didn't like walking around town, never knowing when they might run into each other.

"Anyway," Luke continued, "Carmen's been working really hard on the reception details and I don't want any drama on her big day."

"Isn't it your big day, too?" Elaine asked, reminding both men that she was listening in on their entire conversation.

"Right." Luke took his credit card back and snapped his wallet closed as he jerked his chin toward the exit door. "Let's talk outside."

Elaine had always been one of the biggest gossips in Sugar Falls, even ten years ago. In fact, she was the one who'd first told him that Hannah was cheating on him with Carter Mahoney. Isaac knew all too well she hadn't changed much over the years, so he eagerly followed Luke outside to the front steps of the theater. The exit doors couldn't slam closed fast enough.

"Looks like we're going to get an early snowfall this year, after all," Luke said as he zipped up his jacket against the evening mountain air. "Too bad—I was kind of enjoying that warm spell."

"Did you want me to come out here to talk about the weather or were you planning to explain why you had to blow eight hundred dollars to keep your wedding drama free?"

More importantly, why would Luke think that Isaac would bring any drama in the first place? If he was that worried, Isaac would simply decline the invitation and stay home. He was about to say as much when Luke finally responded.

"Hannah hasn't quite been herself since she got back from Ghana."

Isaac studied the man before him, wishing for a further explanation that didn't seem to be forthcoming. "Not that I would know how the adult version of Hannah Gregson is normally, but I'd imagine that recently adopting a child, especially one from a foreign country who isn't accustomed to life over here, would cause her some added stress."

"Obviously. Plus there's our mom's health that has her worried." Luke shrugged, leaving Isaac to wonder what was going on with Mrs. Gregson. "But finding out that her old flame now lives in the same small town probably hasn't helped much, either."

"Old flame? I'd hardly call—"

"Please." Luke held up a palm. "Let's not pretend like you guys didn't used to be totally bonkers about each other. She didn't eat for a whole week after that video came out."

Isaac flinched. That damn video was one of his deepest regrets and he wished to hell that he and the rest of the world could put the stupid moment behind them. But, other than blaming the foolish and reckless teenager he used to be, there was no defense for the words he'd once spoken. Clearly, there was no point in rehashing his mistake. Instead, he argued, "Maybe Hannah's hunger strike wasn't because of me. I'm pretty sure it was right about that time that people were protesting—"

Luke cut him off again. "She was in love with you back then, and judging by your heated words in that video, you cared pretty deeply for her, too."

Isaac hunched his shoulders against the chilling wind that had picked up, shoving his fists into his pockets. There was no point in denying anything that had taken place that final summer. It wasn't that Isaac was still bitter about things, it was just that seeing her had brought up all the old hurt. It had also stirred to life a lot of the good memories, too.

"So, how are we supposed to get past all that and go on with our lives?" Isaac voiced the same concern that had popped into his head when he saw Hannah for the first time a couple of weeks ago.

"That's the million-dollar question. So here's what I figure… If you and Hannah could talk things out and come to some sort of understanding before my wedding, it would ease a lot of tension. For everyone." Luke took a deep breath. "I thought maybe you could discuss it over dinner at the VFW thing tomorrow."

Isaac's brows lowered with suspicion. "Or you could just ask me not to come to the wedding. It wouldn't hurt my feelings and it'd be a helluva lot cheaper than the eight hundred bucks you just paid."

"Yeah, I thought of that. The easy way out would be all fine and good until the next big town event when you and Hannah have to see each other. You can't just keep avoiding one another like this and pretending you're over things. Hannah would kill me for telling you this, but the whole unresolved situation is eating away at her. And I don't like to see my little sister suffering."

"Suffering?" Isaac grumbled then cleared his throat. "Maybe Carter Mahoney could help ease some of her suffering. Again."

Luke responded by lifting one side of his mouth into a half smile. "I wonder what ol' Carter's up to these days."

Probably still making the moves on someone else's girl, Isaac thought, swallowing a growl.

"Anyway, the bottom line is, I need you two to kiss and make up…" Luke paused, then his face grew more serious. "Scratch that. Just make up—kissing optional—before my wedding so that Hannah doesn't accidentally shove you into the four-tiered cake Carmen's Aunt Lupe is making from scratch."

"You seem to think that anything I could say would convince your sister to let go of a ten-year-old grudge just like that." Isaac snapped his fingers.

Luke rolled his eyes. "I don't think Hannah's the only one holding on to the grudge."

"I'm going to kill my brother," Hannah said the following evening when she opened the front door to Carmen and the twins.

Neither of her blond, curly-haired nephews seemed particularly fazed by their aunt's announcement and brushed past her into the cabin where Sammy was learning to play chess with Hannah's father. Caden asked, "Hey, Pop Pop, where's Grammie?"

Hannah's annoyance with Luke quickly vanished when she heard the question and she held her breath, waiting for her dad to take the lead on what they were going to tell the kids.

"Grammie was feeling pretty tired today so she's at our house in Boise resting and I'm going to babysit all of you little squirts so your parents can have a much-deserved night out. Now, since you two beat me out of three dollars last time we played poker, I decided that we're going to be learning a gentleman's game tonight, instead."

That was the thing about Hannah's dad. Jerry Gregson, a retired youth minister, was always direct and honest, even with young children who didn't quite understand that their grandmother had Stage 3 breast cancer. But he also knew how to relate to kids and, more importantly, how to distract them from asking more questions.

Still, the reminder of her mom's illness sent waves of guilt pouring through Hannah and she wished she had insisted on being at her family's home tonight, taking care of her mother instead of going on a fake date with her ex-boyfriend to the VFW hall. But Donna Gregson was as stubborn as they came and had not only told Hannah to go on the date, she'd volunteered her husband as the sole babysitter of the Gregson clan—a job that several teenagers, two teachers and even the town's sweet, patient librarian wouldn't touch with a ten-foot pole—and claimed that all she needed was a quiet evening with nobody fussing over her.

Of course, that didn't stop Hannah from worrying.

Carmen gave Pop Pop some last-minute instructions about curbing the twins' sugar intake and limiting their video game time while Hannah kissed Sammy goodbye and promised to be home in two hours.

"Two hours?" Carmen asked when they got into her small SUV.

"Or less." Hannah buckled her seat belt. "There's no way I can be in the same room with Isaac Jones longer than that, let alone sit at the same table with him. My brother should've known better."

"I don't blame you for being mad at Luke." Carmen put the car into gear. "I almost killed him myself when I found out how much he paid for Isaac at the bachelor auction."

"Oh, my gosh!" Hannah gasped, realizing that she'd never asked. The auction had barely concluded when she'd found out about the date at Patrelli's Italian Restaurant when she was picking up a pizza last night. Even now she squeezed her eyes shut and shuddered at the way

Mrs. Patrelli had given her a big hug and told her how happy she was that Hannah was finally forgiving Isaac.

It had taken three phone calls and the entire drive back to the cabin to get the basic details that her brother Luke had bid on Isaac to be her date at tonight's fundraiser. Then it had taken another thirty minutes of venting and a lengthy text session with Drew, Luke's twin and a Navy psychologist, to convince Hannah that if she didn't go tonight, the gossips would be out in full force tomorrow morning.

Squinting one eye open, Hannah looked across the interior of the car. "How much did he pay?"

But Carmen's lips were sealed. Probably because Hannah's soon-to-be sister-in-law knew better than to get her any more riled up than she already was. "Don't worry. I'll sit between you and Isaac and run interference the whole night if you want. In fact, that's why I'm picking you up and we're meeting Luke at the hall. He's probably already there now, talking to Isaac and telling him that the whole thing was a practical joke gone bad."

"Is that what it was?" Hannah asked, a familiar ache blossoming in her lower chest. Normally she didn't care what people thought of her, but it hurt when someone she loved played her for a fool. "A practical joke?"

Carmen sighed. "No, it wasn't a joke. But if I tell you why Luke did it, you have to promise not to go off on him when you see him."

Hannah studied Carmen through the dim light inside the car as they made their way down the dark highway and toward the center of Sugar Falls. "I don't think that's a promise I could keep."

Luckily, Carmen either hadn't heard, or had decided not to require a vow. "Your brother's really worried about having the wedding go smoothly and thinks that if you see Isaac there and haven't worked things out by then, then someone might say the wrong thing and he just doesn't want any unnecessary commotion."

"Seriously?" Hannah clenched her fingers and had to remind her lungs to force all the air she was inhaling back out. "He thinks *I'm* going to be the one to cause a scene? And about Isaac Jones, of all people?"

"If you breathe any harder, I'm going to have to turn on the defroster. Besides, I said a commotion. Not a scene. Luke's more worried about emotions running high and the *potential* for drama. I saw you at the jog-a-thon after Elaine and Marcia were talking to you. Can you honestly say that if one of those bitchy gossips tried to start up with you about Isaac, that you wouldn't get worked up? And if *you're* miserable at the wedding, then your mom will be miserable and…"

Carmen didn't have to finish. Nobody liked to think about Donna Gregson's condition, let alone mention it out loud. However, with their mom's refusal of any more treatment, this could possibly be one of their last major family celebrations with her, and Hannah could understand why Luke would want to make it extra special. Hell, they all wanted to make things extra special for their mother. So if that meant that she had to paste a smile on her face and play nice with Isaac, then that's what Hannah would do.

Unfortunately, when she walked into the VFW hall ten minutes later, Hannah's stomach was in knots and her heart was beating so loudly she could hear her own pulse thumping in her ears over the sound of the eighties song coming from the band on the small raised platform near the dance floor. It was a good thing Big Rhonda and the Roadsters usually played gigs at the VFW on Saturday nights. They'd only had a couple of weeks to come up with and rehearse a new playlist for tonight's theme.

Hannah didn't get dressed up very often and she tugged at the short hem of the dress she'd borrowed from Drew's wife. Her sister-in-law Kylie had an eye for fashion and an aversion to loose-fitting clothes. The soft, silky material and floral print hadn't seemed so daring when it was on the hanger, but now that it was clinging to Hannah's hips, she was reluctant to leave her bulky jacket at the coat check.

It didn't help that everyone was looking in her direction as she followed Carmen toward the round table where Luke and Drew were sitting with Kylie. There was another couple seated with them, but Hannah's eyes couldn't focus on anybody other than the man standing behind an empty chair, holding a bottle of beer and frowning at the dance floor as though it might swallow him whole if he dared to take a step in the wrong direction.

Right. Isaac had always hated dancing, especially in front of people. He'd once told Hannah that his mom had made him go to cotillion classes and the overly technical steps of the waltz had emotionally scarred him for life.

Some of the tension in Hannah's muscles loosened as she recognized the uneasiness in Isaac's body language. After all this time, she shouldn't still be able to recognize those tiny details, but maybe she could use her knowledge and his discomfort to her advantage. Not that she *wanted* the guy to be uncomfortable. But if she could get her emotions under control and act as though she was completely unbothered by the fact that he was there—or that her brother had literally paid money to ensure his presence—then at least Hannah wouldn't be the most awkward person in the room.

Straightening her shoulders, she told herself that she would just need to fake it for two hours. The problem was that she'd never been a very good actress.

Chapter Seven

"This is supposed to be a dinner dance," Hannah yelled above the music almost three hours later. "Where's the dinner part?"

Isaac shrugged. They were the only people left at their table when the band began playing "Beat It" and everyone else had made a mad rush toward the dance floor. But there was no way he was going to follow suit.

"You want me to go get you another drink?" he offered.

He'd already reached his maximum alcohol level for the night, and the last thing he needed was more beer. But if it kept him from sitting here all alone with Hannah Gregson, then he'd gladly head to the bar for another round.

She shook her head, her long, loose hair falling behind her shoulders. "If I have any more wine on an empty stomach, someone's going to have to use a wheelbarrow to push me out of here."

"Ha." Isaac barked out a laugh, the vibration unfamiliar in his throat since he hadn't been able to laugh all evening. "I'd forgotten about that."

The first summer they'd met, Elaine Marconi, who'd been Elaine Simmons back then, had sneaked a couple of six packs of wine coolers from her daddy's mini-mart and brought them on a cleanup hike that Hannah had organized. They were supposed to be picking up litter and other debris that tourists and novice hikers had left behind on the trail going up to the waterfalls.

Hannah had been appalled that there was underage drinking going on at a volunteer event she'd assisted in organizing, but little did she know that the only way to get most of the high school kids there to help out was the promise of a good time. Hannah had been even more appalled when Elaine had passed out and Chuck Marconi had grabbed an old wheelbarrow from the back of his grandfather's pickup truck to get her back down the trail. Isaac smiled at the memory of how scandalized Hannah'd been and how that evening, when he'd driven her home, she'd told him that what she liked most about him was that he hadn't gotten into the alcohol like the other kids in town. He'd stayed clearheaded and on mission.

"Looks like Elaine still can't hold her wine," Hannah said, nodding toward the dance floor where the woman was doing a very bad impression of a trout trying to swim upstream. "Not that I should talk, but I'm pretty sure everyone's going to need some food soon to absorb all the booze."

"Keep in mind that Cessy and Freckles organized this event," Isaac offered, actually pleased that Hannah was finally starting to relax and make cordial conversation with him. "They're probably going to try to sell as many raffle tickets as they can before they serve dinner. The more people have to drink, the freer they are with their wallets."

"Was my brother drinking when he bid on you?" Her tone was playful, but her direct gaze put Isaac on edge.

"Not as far as I could tell. But then again, I didn't even know he was there, let alone what he was doing until Freckles yelled *sold*."

"Don't worry," Hannah said with a dismissive wave of her hand. "I'm not going to hold you responsible for what he did."

Isaac wanted to ask her why she was holding him responsible for everything else. However, in the interest of not steering them down the path of painful memories, he bit his tongue.

"But I am curious to know how much he paid for you to sit here with me."

"Nobody had to pay me to sit here with you," Isaac said, surprising himself with the honest admission.

"Obviously the money wasn't for you. It went to charity and all that." And a new brush truck for his department since they'd beat out the police officers for total amount of bids.

"No, Hannah. I mean, nobody had to pay any money to anyone. I would've gladly sat here with you if you would've just asked."

"Yeah, right." She made a sputter that could've been a hiccup, then lowered her eyes as she played with the stem of her empty glass. "Except I would've had too much pride to ever ask."

"I know," he agreed. Her pride and her determination were the things that had first attracted Isaac to her. And her refusal to come clean with him after the night of the bonfire had been their downfall. "That's why your brother paid all that money. In the hopes that we'd get on speaking terms again."

"Which brings me back to my original question." Hannah looked up and her clear blue gaze sent a ripple down his spine. "How much?"

Isaac finished off the rest of his beer and jiggled the empty bottle. "If we're going to talk about this, I'm going to need a little more liquid courage. Want one?"

"Fine." Her metal folding chair screeched against the hardwood floor as she scooted back. It didn't help that the song had just ended so everyone within a hundred-foot radius heard the sound and turned in their direction as they made their way to the bar.

Thankfully there was no line and he was able to order their drinks instead of gawking like a schoolboy at her long, bare legs.

"I really wish people would stop staring at us," Hannah yelled into his ear when the music resumed. "It's as if they think we're about to go into a UFC cage fight at any second and spar to the death."

"It'd help if you weren't shooting daggers at me every time we see each other around town," Isaac replied.

"I'm not shooting daggers!" Hannah huffed, drawing his attention to the V-neck of her dress. "I'm indifferent. Besides, what about the way you're always staring at me?"

Isaac smiled. "If you were really indifferent, you wouldn't notice me staring at you at all."

She returned his smile and a throb of awareness raced through him. "So, you admit that you've been staring at me?"

"I'll freely admit that I stare at you, Hannah Gregson. You're still the prettiest woman I've ever laid eyes on."

For the first time he could remember, he'd shocked

Hannah into silence. Her glass of wine was halfway to her parted pink lips and her head was tilted to one side. The confusion marring her normally smooth brow would've been comical if he hadn't been so aware of how close she was or how her perfume smelled like the wild jasmine growing on the side of Jonesy's log house.

Okay, so maybe he wouldn't have admitted that he was still attracted to her if he'd been in his right mind. But the band was playing that slow song from *Top Gun* and Isaac had always been a sucker for military movies. He reached out and drew her hand toward him. "Come on and dance with me."

Both of her perfectly arched brows lifted. "Since when do you like dancing, Isaac Jones?"

"Since twenty seconds ago when you finally smiled at me."

"Fine," Hannah said for the second time, her face flushing slightly, and he didn't waste a minute leading her toward the crowded dance floor. On the way, he paused only long enough to take her glass and set it down on an empty table next to his full bottle of beer. The second his boots hit the parquet floor, he turned to pull her into his arms.

It was like coming home, the way her body pressed up against his. Her hands were stiff on his shoulders for the first few beats, then gently eased behind his neck. She didn't pull back when he allowed his own palms to slide to the spot just below her waist. He used his thumb to stroke her lower spine. Isaac dipped his mouth to her ear and whispered, "I remember when your hair was so long, it reached all the way down to here."

Because their faces were so close, he couldn't see her response. But if she recalled that the only time she'd let her hair loose in front of him was the night they'd made love, then he could well imagine the blush that was likely staining her cheeks right that second.

Unfortunately, that was also the exact second that Uncle Jonesy danced Mae Johnston, the mayor's wife, near them and the older woman patted Hannah's shoulder and said, "Now that the two of you are finally getting along, can I count on you both to head up the Thanksgiving canned food drive this year?"

Hannah's head only moved an inch or two away from Isaac, but fortunately her body didn't stop swaying when she replied. "Well, you know that you can always count on me, Mrs. Johnston."

"That's what I figured. How about you, Chief? Three years ago when Hannah led the charge, we brought in enough groceries to feed fifty local families. I'm sure if you co-chair the event with her, we could raise almost double that amount."

Isaac didn't take his eyes off Hannah's face when he replied, "I'm game if she is."

Her chin dipped down as she shyly grinned and his heart lifted. He couldn't believe it. Not only were they getting along, they'd also just agreed to work together.

"Good for you two." Mrs. Johnston's tight gray curls didn't so much as wobble as she nodded her head vigorously. The woman was obviously so pleased with herself for recruiting them, she didn't even bother to lower her voice when she added, "If you ask me, getting you guys back together was probably the best eight hundred dollars Luke Gregson ever spent."

And just like that, alarms went off in Isaac's brain, but it was too late. Hannah's body went completely still and all the warmth left her eyes. Her hands dropped from his neck to her hips and her voice was no longer playful.

"Eight hundred dollars?"

* * *

Hannah was still reeling from the shock of how much money Luke had bid in order to make Isaac act civilly to her. She was also still reeling from how close she'd let the man get to her at the VFW dance. One minute, they couldn't even look at each other. The next, they were slow dancing and she'd practically plastered her body against his.

She groaned as she sank into one of the blue plastic chairs at the U-shaped table in the back of her empty classroom the following Monday morning. It had been two days and Hannah could still feel the hard ridges of his chest muscles against her breasts.

Stop, she commanded herself. *You're letting yourself get all goo-goo over Isaac Jones again.*

It wasn't like it was Isaac's fault that Luke had spent a fortune to try and make them get along. But the whole thing had left her feeling as if the joke was on her and all she'd wanted was to get the hell out of there. Luckily, dinner had been served directly after the song—as well as the short-lived truce—ended, and Hannah was able to make her goodbyes and get home to Sammy before the dancing resumed. Too bad she hadn't left before Mae Johnston had suckered her into heading up this canned food drive with Isaac.

In fact, Mrs. Johnston hadn't even waited twenty-four hours before sending both Hannah and Isaac a text reminding them of their commitment and suggesting they meet that week to strategize. Hannah had ignored the message, but now it was Monday morning and her class was out to recess. She needed to get this over with.

Forcing herself to her feet, she walked over to her desk. When she pulled her phone out of the center drawer,

Hannah frowned at the notification of a new text message in a separate thread.

There was no name, because it wasn't from someone in her contacts. But she was pretty sure she recognized the number from the text Mrs. Johnston had sent the previous night. She opened up the message and saw the smiling face of her son sitting in the fire engine. Underneath the picture was the typed message, Looks like I got your phone number after all.

Yep, it was Isaac. Hannah's tummy did a little flip and her fingers twitched over the electronic keyboard as she pondered how she should reply. She couldn't very well ignore him. But she also didn't think it was a good idea for them to become texting buddies. She couldn't trust herself on a very public dance floor with the man when there was an audience watching them. How was she going to trust herself in a private conversation where she could hide her physical response behind a screen?

No. Letting her guard down around him was way too dangerous for her own peace of mind. Two nights ago, all it had taken was a couple of glasses of wine and a compliment and she was practically putty in his hands again.

Resolved to put some distance between them without sounding like she was avoiding him, she opted for a polite reply.

Thank you for the picture. Sammy will love it. She pushed Send, then tried to be as businesslike as possible with a follow-up message to let him know where they stood.

Thank you for volunteering to help with the food drive. I'm sure you're busy and I'm more than happy to handle it on my own so you can feel free to bow out gracefully.

She was about to switch her phone off when she saw a bubble appear on the screen, indicating that he was typing a response. Hannah glanced at the clock on the wall above her whiteboard. She still had ten minutes until the bell rang, so she tried to grade Elsa Folsom's makeup book report instead of staring anxiously at her phone. But she couldn't get past the title, *How to Train Your Dragon*.

When her phone finally vibrated, so did her heart.

Until she saw what he'd written.

Afraid that it's too late, no matter how graceful I am. Mrs. Johnston was in the fire station first thing this morning to make sure I hadn't forgotten. But if you aren't comfortable with us being on the same committee, I totally understand if you want to back out.

Was he issuing some sort of challenge? Like he didn't think she would be willing to work with him? This time, her fingers flew over the keypad.

Seriously, I could organize a canned food drive in my sleep. I really don't need your help. I'm sure your volunteer efforts would be better served on a different project. I hear the library is trying to raise funds for a new teen room...

Nice try, Gregson. But I already made a commitment. Besides, I don't mind doing both the food drive and the library thing if it's too much for you.

A blast of air rushed out of Hannah's nostrils, causing them to flare. Why was she suddenly feeling like the fire-breathing dragon in the picture on the cover of Elsa's book report? Because she was *not* going to work with Isaac Jones, no matter how good the cause.

But instead of telling him as much, she typed, It's not too much for me.

Good. We should probably meet soon to go over strategies and job assignments.

Hannah set the phone down and stepped away from her desk to force herself to think. Needing something else to do besides stare at the screen, she rewrapped the bun on top of her head, pulling a little tighter than normal and jabbing a dull pencil into her hair to secure it in place. *She* was the one who should be suggesting the meeting. His saying it first made it seem like he was taking command. And there was no way she was taking a back seat to him.

Her fingers tapped on the letters furiously. We can meet later today.

There. Now she was calling the shots.

Where? he asked.

As she looked around her classroom, she thought *why not?* It was her turf and it was a semipublic place, which meant that everyone from town wouldn't be watching them, but there would still be the potential for other teachers to stop by, so they weren't completely alone, either. At the school. 3:00.

School was over at 2:30, so that would give her a thirty-minute window to run to the restroom, fix her hair and maybe find an old tube of lip gloss somewhere in her purse. If not, Nurse Dunn always had an arsenal of lipstick colors she wore and probably wouldn't mind loaning…

No! She was not going to primp or otherwise get ready to see Isaac. Or any man, for that matter.

The bell rang right as her phone buzzed with his response.

I'll still be on duty then and our monthly training class for volunteers won't wrap up until 3. Bring Sammy over to the station after school and we can talk here.

There? To the fire station? Not that she could blame the guy for not wanting to come to the school again. Last time he was there, she'd dumped an entire cup of red Gatorade down the front of his shirt, which would've been funny if she hadn't been so mad at Elaine and Marcia at the time.

But then he'd pulled her into that tight hug and made that comment about her owing him ice cream still.

Her smirk faded as a spiral of unease wound its way through her belly. It was pretty ballsy of him to tell her to come to *his* place of employment. And then order her to bring her son with her? The guy had a lot of nerve.

Her students trickled into the classroom and Hannah was prevented from writing back an excuse. But oh, man, were there plenty of things she would've liked to say to him about his high-handed ways. As soon as she had more time, she knew exactly what she would reply.

Unfortunately, there was a surprise visit from the district superintendent at lunch to give the annoying PTA secretary—the woman who'd warned Elaine to stop talking when Hannah approached them at the jog-a-thon—an award for best kiss-up or number one henchman or some such nonsense.

Then Hannah's class had to go to the computer lab and learn about a new math program online, but none of the kids could figure out how to log on because their passwords and usernames had gotten transposed. Later, Elsa Folsom had to give a presentation on her book report and, because the other kids had already done theirs when she was absent, the girl was way too nervous to speak in front of the class.

Hannah spent at least fifteen minutes trying to coax Elsa out from where she'd hidden in the coatroom. Hannah was already way off her schedule the last hour of the day when the art teacher showed up unannounced with a slew of messy colored chalk that got all over the desks and carpets.

She'd ended up being far too busy to reply to Isaac, which was probably for the best, because by the time all her students were out the door, Hannah had convinced herself that Sammy would love going to the fire station. Plus, her son would be the perfect buffer to keep her from getting too irrational in front of Isaac.

After all, if she was going to have to be on his turf, she might as well take reinforcements.

Chapter Eight

As it turned out, Hannah took four reinforcements to the fire station that afternoon. Luke had called her to say he was running late and asked if she could bring Aiden and Caden home from school that day. She had just agreed when Carmen had called and said that Luke had forgotten Choogie Nguyen, the twins' best friend, was supposed to be coming to their house, as well.

She'd never had Choogie in one of her classes, but she knew the boy was in the gifted program. To say that he was a talkative kid was an extreme understatement. The current noise level in her car was deafening, as all of the children talked about their favorite Pokemon characters and gave a detailed, catalogued inventory of every single YouTube video they'd ever seen.

Well, all of the children except Sammy. Her son sat in the middle of the back seat, eyes wide open and lips firmly shut as he absorbed everything his cousins and their friend were saying. Sammy was younger and still somewhat shy in group situations and, in his typical fashion, he stayed quiet and observed everything he could about the children around him. Hannah hoped that pretty soon he would feel comfortable enough to participate.

"Did they have Pokemon where you came from?" Choogie was fully turned around in the front seat, his seat belt stretched out as he spoke to Sammy.

Hannah held her breath, trying to catch her son's gaze in the rearview mirror. She remembered another teacher complaining that Choogie was a handful in class, one of those children who was way smarter than everyone else and got bored easily. But she couldn't recall hearing anything about whether or not he was a mean-spirited kid. Her knuckles whitened as she gripped the steering wheel and waited to intervene if the conversation took an insulting turn.

"Yes, but just the shows," Sammy said in his soft voice. "I didn't have the cards."

Choogie hooked an arm around the headrest and Hannah had to remind him to face forward. But sixty seconds later, the boy was turned around again. "You speak English really good. How long did it take you to learn it after you got here?"

A dull ache started in her chest and she was about to tell Choogie to face forward again, but her son's voice stopped her.

"English is the official language of Ghana and that's what we spoke at the children's home where I used to live." Sammy was used to having to give this response and he usually just left it at that. However, today he added, "I can also speak Akan, though, because most of the people in our village use it at the market and stuff."

"That's cool. I was born in China and came to America when I was still a baby so I grew up learning English. One of my moms speaks Vietnamese and she taught me some words, but we don't really speak it at home. Unless my grandpa comes to visit."

Hannah felt her shoulders relax against the driver's seat. She was so on edge lately, expecting the worst from everyone, she'd totally forgotten that Choogie was adopted. His situation wasn't exactly the same as Sammy's, and the boy was a few years older, but maybe it would be good for Sammy to know that he wasn't the only one in town with a unique family.

"Do you guys know any bad words in a different language?" Aiden asked a bit too eagerly as they pulled into the parking lot behind the public safety building next to City Hall. "Our new mom speaks Spanish and one time I heard her say—"

"No bad words," Hannah interrupted, then pointed at all four boys, making sure she got a solemn nod of understanding from each. Although Sammy's expression was more puzzled than anything else, and she made a mental note to have a separate talk with him about it tonight when they got home. The last thing she needed was for some parents to complain that their children were learning profanities from her son at school. Or from her nephews, for that matter.

"Now, when we go inside the fire station, how are we going to behave?"

"Like gentlemen," the boys all repeated in unison. She'd given them this lecture before they'd even left the school grounds.

"Are we going to ask a million questions?"

"No," they said.

"Are we going to climb on the trucks or try on the firefighters' clothes without permission?"

"No."

She racked her brain for any other possible shenanigans her nephews could get up to. Remembering a time when she'd taken the boys for swim lessons at the YMCA in Boise, she added, "Are we going to sneak into their locker room and turn on all the shower nozzles at once to create a sauna?"

"How do you know they even have showers?" Caden asked. "Have you been in them? Does Chief Jones allow girls in the boys' locker room?"

Hannah's cheeks heated at the sudden thought of seeing Isaac in the shower. Of seeing just how muscular and broad his chest had become since she'd last seen it bare. Blowing a strand of loose hair off her forehead, Hannah sighed. "They have female firefighters, so I'm sure the ladies have their own locker room. And you may not sneak into there, either."

"Fine," Aiden drawled out. "No locker rooms."

As they walked toward the entrance to the fire station, Hannah gave one last directive. "Remember that I'm here for a meeting with Chief Jones. The quicker I get done, the quicker we can go to Noodie's Ice Cream Shoppe for sundaes."

The three older boys cheered, but Sammy didn't seem as excited about her exit strategy. Probably because, if it were up to her son, he'd move into the firehouse and never leave.

Ever since Hannah'd arrived at the orphanage in Ghana, Sammy had always wanted to remain close to her side— unless he was running somewhere. But now Isaac was the one her son wanted to follow around. Too bad Hannah wasn't going to be there more than twenty minutes.

Forty-five minutes after Hannah arrived with her quartet of curious boys, Isaac was finally able to get her alone in his office and bring up the canned food drive. He leaned back in his chair as he spoke. "So, I figured we could put up some flyers, drop a few donation boxes around town, then deliver it all to the food bank before Thanksgiving."

But Hannah was barely paying him the slightest bit of attention as her neck twisted to look down the hall. "Are you sure the kids are okay in the kitchen with Jonesy and Scooter?"

Isaac followed the direction of her gaze. Due to department staffing needs, the volunteer firefighters still came in to cover the occasional shift or to attend trainings. It was a blessed coincidence that the two older guys were also great with keeping kids busy. Isaac himself was a prime example of their patience with high energy youth. "Sure. My uncle will keep them in line. Besides, what's the worst they can do in there? Start a fire?"

But Hannah didn't laugh.

"See, that was a joke because we're in a fire station surrounded by firefighters—"

"Maybe we should talk someplace where my nephews are within eyesight."

Isaac sighed in frustration and leaned back in his desk chair. He'd been around the Gregson twins long enough to know that Hannah was probably right. But all he needed was five minutes in his office with her undivided attention. Then she could be on her way and this whole food drive would practically be over before they knew it.

Which meant working with her would soon be over. Isaac wasn't sure how to feel about that. After their dance at the VFW Hall, he was no longer quite so eager to avoid her. But then she'd sent those text messages earlier today implying she was still eager to avoid *him*.

"Hannah, the boys are fine. It'll take longer to get this knocked out if I have to answer any more questions about dalmatians. Or how hot a fire would have to be to char a zombie. Or why we need to have showers in the locker rooms here at the station."

A pink blush stole up Hannah's cheeks, the same one that had appeared when he'd explained to Caden that the firefighters were on duty for twenty-four-hour shifts and so the fire station had to be like a second home for them.

Isaac lifted his chin and studied her. The only reason a woman would blush like that when talking about showers was if she was thinking about *who* was taking one. He felt a knowing smile playing at the corners his lips.

He stacked his hands behind his head as though he was perfectly at ease and relaxed, and not at all thinking about getting her naked in a shower—which he was. However, the motion drew her attention to his biceps and he felt the heat of her stare on his upper arms. He was tempted to flex his muscles—just enough to show off. After all, he'd worked hard enough to get them to look like this; he might as well enjoy impressing her with them. But the way she was staring was equally arousing, proving that their attraction to each other was still strong and still very much mutual.

As rewarding as the realization was, a kernel of doubt gnawed at the back of his mind, reminding him of the last time he'd given in to that attraction. Could he let himself get close to her a second time and risk all that pain and heartbreak again?

He looked at the blond bun twisted on the top of her head. He'd been haunted by that long silky hair for years after they broke up. How many times had he thought he'd seen Hannah on the campus at Yale or on a street in San Antonio when he'd initially been stationed at Fort Sam

Houston, only to catch up to the woman with similar hair and find out it was a stranger?

No. He couldn't go through all of that again. Or, at least, he shouldn't. Isaac brought his hands down, clasped his fingers in front of his stomach and watched as Hannah gave a slight shake of her head, probably coming back to her senses, as well.

"Right," she said in a throaty voice, before attempting a discreet cough. "You mentioned flyers and collection boxes. We'll need both of those, but there's a little more to it than that."

"There always is a little more to it with you," Isaac murmured.

"What's that?"

Isaac cleared his throat. "What else do we need?"

"Well, we need to set dates. And we have to call the local businesses to see who's willing to have a box to collect the goods. Then we'll want a social media presence so we can reach out to everyone who doesn't see the flyers or needs a little more reminding. To be honest, I feel like we're already cutting it close with only ten days until Thanksgiving. The families who are counting on the food will want to know what they're getting in advance so they can plan their meals."

Nodding, Isaac had to concede that she really didn't need him. The woman could, in fact, organize this event in her sleep. But he wasn't about to admit as much.

"Hmm. What else?" Hannah tapped her chin as she reached across his desk and grabbed the lined notebook he'd tossed there after the training class. She pulled her lower lip between her teeth as she began writing out a list.

Isaac took advantage of the opportunity to blatantly study the woman who still had the power to make his pulse race just as quickly as it had when he'd been an eighteen-year-old, inexperienced youth. That soft, blond hair he'd dreamed about was falling out of the messy bun atop her head and her slender fingers scribbled furiously, making the muscles in her forearm flex.

He was so deep in a trance, remembering the way those same arms had been wrapped around his neck a couple of nights ago, that he didn't realize she'd stopped writing until he heard the paper tear in half.

"Here. This is your to-do list." She handed him one long strip, her fingers brushing against his. A current of heat ricocheted through him and he lost his grip, causing the paper to flutter down to his desktop. His arm was still extended toward her, yet he purposely waited for Hannah to retrieve the list, and this time he paid closer attention to her face when she passed it to him. Isaac needed to see if she had the same reaction to his touch as he did to hers. He also might've used his thumb to stroke slowly along her palm, tracing a light path to her wrist.

The quivering of her bottom lip was ever so slight, but there was no way for her to disguise the scarlet color stealing up her cheeks as she stared at their joined hands. Yep, proud and headstrong Hannah Gregson was definitely flustered and a little turned on. Isaac's chest expanded and the sheet of paper again fell to his desk.

Hannah blinked several times before yanking her hand back. She made a move to pick up the list again, but must've thought better of it because she snatched the matching one closer to her, instead. She cleared her throat, but her voice was still raspy when she said, "And this one is mine. If you get too busy or bored or don't have time or whatever, just let me know and I can cover for you."

At that, Hannah stood up and made a hasty exit, her tote bag bouncing against her rounded hip as she made her way back to the kitchen to collect her boys and leave without so much as a goodbye. Or an *I told you so.*

Looking around at the chocolate batter spilled all over the industrial kitchen counters, Hannah would've loved nothing more than to round up the four kids and head straight to the car, leaving the mess for someone else to clean. It didn't help that her pulse was still throbbing, each beat pulsating against her left wrist where Isaac's thumb had touched her skin moments ago. Unfortunately, an alarm on the wall let out a shrieking wail and the walkie-talkies attached to the firefighters' belts crackled to life.

Everyone in the station, including the boys, went into hyperdrive as they abandoned their mixing bowls and stirring spoons and ran toward the apparatus bay where the trucks were parked and the equipment stored. Hannah raced to keep up, not that there was anything she could do to help the firefighters or the paramedics besides keeping the overly inquisitive children out of their way.

Oxygen pumped into her chest and adrenaline rushed through her veins as she entered the enormous garage-style area just as the sally port door was rolling up. Relief poured through her as she counted four small heads quietly lined up beside the bench where Isaac was stepping into his boots and turnout gear.

When she arrived next to them, she heard the tail end of Isaac's instructions to the boys. Something about not enough room for them in the fire engine this time.

"Should we follow in our aunt's car?" Aiden asked eagerly.

"Nah. We'll be back before you know it. The dispatcher thinks it's just Mrs. Alvarez's oven catching fire again." Isaac turned in Hannah's direction, his expression not showing the least amount of concern. "This happens every time Duncan's Market has a sale on frozen pizzas. Mrs. Alvarez always forgets to remove the cardboard sheet underneath before baking them."

Hannah nodded silently, but her eyes were probably as round as Sammy's. Although, her son's eyes were wide with wonder and excitement whereas Hannah's were filled with worry. Mrs. Alvarez's granddaughter Monica, the town librarian, had been worried about the older woman showing signs of dementia. Hannah sent up a quick prayer that the fire wasn't anything too serious.

Isaac climbed into the front passenger seat—she recalled from their tour forty-five minutes ago that the seat had a special name but she'd been too busy watching Isaac's full lips move as he'd talked to pay attention—and he shot the boys a thumbs-up as the diesel engine roared.

Samuel held up his own smaller thumb, and Hannah put a protective arm around his shoulder. His little six-year-old body was all but vibrating with anticipation as the siren switched on and the fire engine rolled out.

"We'll close the garage door for you," Choogie called out—unnecessarily, as the door had already begun its rolling descent behind the paramedics' truck.

She was left standing there. Alone in a fire station with four boys and no clue about what to do when the crew left on a call. Hannah pulled her cell out of her tote bag and sent a text message to Carmen, whose police department was on the other side of the building. Should they stay put? Should they let themselves out? Although that would be quite the adventure because they would have to wind their way through several empty hallways to find the same door they'd come in.

Instead of a beeping from her phone indicating a reply text, Hannah heard a beeping come from the other side of the wall. Caden jumped off the bench. "The cake's ready!"

She followed the boys to the kitchen, relieved that someone had had the foresight to turn off the stove before responding to the alarm. She took the cake out of the oven, then, surveying the disaster all over the counters, Hannah knew that she couldn't very well leave the chocolate batter mess for the crew to come back to.

"Let's try and finish in here and clean up," she said, pulling the sleeves of her sweater up to her elbows. Hannah's nose wrinkled at the big pot of spaghetti sauce no longer simmering on the stove. Should it be lumpy like that?

Giving each of the boys a task, she set to work boiling some water for the noodles so that the firefighters would have a nice dinner to come home to. The twins were at the sink, shoulder deep in soapy water, when Carmen finally walked in.

"Mom!" the twins yelled in unison, and Hannah's heart melted at how easily her nephews had taken to their soon-to-be stepmother. In fact, they had been the ones to set Luke and Carmen up in the first place. Glancing at Sammy, who was frosting the cake, Hannah wondered if his calling her Mama came just as easily to him.

"I got off duty and swung by the dispatcher's desk on the way over here." Carmen spoke quietly to Hannah after she'd been wrapped in two sudsy hugs. "The blaze turned out to be bigger than usual and took out an entire wall in her kitchen."

"How's Mrs. Alvarez?" Hannah bit her lips, not wanting to ask about Isaac although she suspected her eyes begged for any information about him, as well. "Is anyone hurt?"

"Nobody got hurt. In fact, Mrs. Alvarez was in the

back of the house and so oblivious to the fire that she offered the paramedics some slices of pizza when they were looking her over for injuries. But Monica, her granddaughter, is pretty shook up."

"I can imagine." Hannah blew a loose strand of hair out of her face and wrapped an arm around her waist as though to give her diaphragm permission to take normal breaths.

Carmen took the twins and Choogie away with her, but when Hannah told Sammy it was time for them to leave, her sweet son looked at her with pleading eyes that reflected an edge of nervousness and asked, "Can we stay to make sure that they get back okay?"

Hannah glanced at the clock hanging over the stainless steel stove. She knew that she should say no—that she should stay as far away from Isaac as possible. Obviously, she couldn't trust her body not to respond whenever he was near.

"They might be gone awhile," Hannah bluffed, unsure of how long this type of thing might take. Was there an investigation that would need to be done? Did they have to stay and interview witnesses? Knowing Isaac, he was probably staying longer to help clean up Mrs. Alvarez's kitchen.

"But what if they get back and Chief Jones doesn't know where we went?" Sammy asked.

More like, what if they got back and Chief Jones caught her blushing at him again? She thought of the way his hand had intimately touched her earlier, when she'd passed him the list, and then brightened at her sudden realization. "We can leave him a note!"

Hannah all but skipped to Isaac's office to get the notepad off his desk, but when she returned to the kitchen, her son was completely oblivious to how anxious she was to leave. He insisted on writing the note himself. However, his penmanship—which was normally above average for a kindergartener—wasn't as perfect as he thought it should be.

Sammy was carefully working on his third draft when she heard the rumbling of the diesel engine pulling into the apparatus bay. Hannah looked toward the ceiling as her stomach sank.

So much for making a stealthy getaway before Isaac returned.

Chapter Nine

Isaac spied a late model Prius in the parking lot as Scooter pulled the fire engine into the bay. That same car had been at the station when they'd left, which meant that Hannah was still here. Had she waited for him?

As much as that should've lifted his spirits, he was tired and dirty and had an investigation report to write. He didn't really have time to answer five hundred questions about an oven fire that had gotten out of control. Or to think about how he'd downplayed the seriousness of it when he'd known for a while now that the elderly Mrs. Alvarez shouldn't be staying alone anymore.

While everyone else headed to the showers or their cell phones to call their loved ones, Isaac pulled off his jacket and helmet in the apparatus bay and walked toward the kitchen in his pants and acrid, sweat-stained T-shirt.

Sammy Gregson's catapult hug caught him by total surprise. And, judging from the look on Hannah's face, it also caught the boy's mother by surprise. But Isaac lifted him up, clinging to the boy who'd wrapped his skinny legs and arms around him, the scent of sugary frosting smeared on the kid's sleeve a welcome relief from the smoke he'd been sniffing on his clothes a few moments ago.

"Did you put the fire out?" Sammy asked, his face smooth and serious and at eye level with Isaac's.

"We did. And, more importantly, nobody got hurt."

"So you saved the day?"

"My whole crew saved the day. We worked really well together as a team." Isaac looked around the kitchen, not seeing anyone other than Hannah. "Speaking of teams, where are your cousins and their friend?"

"My Aunt Carmen picked them up and took them home. But I asked Mama if we could stay here and make sure you got back safely."

That explained the emotional welcome—the boy had been worried about him. Sammy's hold loosened and Isaac took that as a sign that he could set the kid down. He chose the spot on the counter next to a rectangular pan filled with something brown and slightly jiggly. "And what's this?"

"That's the cake we were making with Mr. Jonesy and Mr. Scooter. Except, when you guys left, the oven got shut off and it didn't finish cooking."

Hannah gasped. "Oh, my gosh. I had no idea it didn't finish cooking. Sweetie, if you knew it wasn't done, why didn't you tell me?"

"Because your face was doing this." He pushed the skin together over the bridge of his little nose so it made a dramatic crease. "I thought maybe you were scared about the big fire. But when you gave us all jobs to do, your forehead stopped being all wrinkly. So I put the frosting on the cake, just like you told me."

Isaac leaned against the counter, his arm only a few

inches away from hers. He lowered his voice, "Were you really scared?"

She looked a little embarrassed. "I wasn't scared. I was just a bit nervous. That's all."

He grinned. "Nervous that I was going to get hurt?"

"No. Nervous that I was being left alone in the fire station and that one of the kids was going to get into the ax room, or whatever you call that place with all the tools, while you were all gone."

"Sorry to leave you on your own like that, Hannah. Normally, we would leave someone back here, but I told you we were understaffed right now." She nodded, so he added, "But it looks like you kept everyone in line. At least, the kitchen looks better than it did when the alarm went off."

"Well, we cleaned it up. I didn't really know what else to do."

"We also made a salad," Sammy said, opening the huge fridge to reveal a bowl filled with lettuce and vegetables.

Isaac looked toward the stove at the pot filled with plain pasta. "And spaghetti, apparently?"

Hannah shrugged, offering a small smile. "I figured you would need some when you got back."

"Why?" Isaac asked.

"To go with the sauce?"

"What sauce?" Jonesy asked as he walked into the kitchen with Scooter on his heels.

"The spaghetti sauce in the pot," Hannah gestured a thumb toward the stove.

"Girl…" Jonesy shook his head as he *tsked* "…that's my award-winning firehouse chili."

"That explains why there were beans in it," Hannah mumbled.

"Mama isn't so great of a cook," Sammy said in a

whisper that was so loud, even Scooter, who was hard of hearing, heard. "But she's real good at board games and doing voices when she reads me books. And she gives the best hugs."

At least, she does when she thinks nobody's watching, Isaac thought, remembering her quick squeeze at the jog-a-thon.

"Well, we can't very well send you home with a bad cook on an empty belly," Scooter said to her son. "C'mon. Let's go set the table."

"Oh, no. Thank you but we can't..." Hannah's objection died on her lips as she watched Sammy hop down and happily follow the older man out of the kitchen. She turned to Isaac. "Really, we can't stay."

"Tell that to those guys." Isaac jerked his chin toward the dining room.

Jonesy was leaning over the stove sniffing at his chili, probably to make sure Hannah hadn't messed anything up besides the cake. "You didn't add anything to this, did you?"

"Didn't touch it." Hannah rolled her eyes, then lowered her voice as she whispered to Isaac. "I'm not that bad of a cook, you know."

Isaac crossed his arms across his chest as he smiled at her. "Really? What was the last thing you made for dinner that you didn't pull out of the freezer?"

"Does cereal count?"

"Only if you're eight years old."

"Hmph." She crossed her own arms, mimicking his stance. "You'd be lucky to have a bowl of my cereal, Isaac Jones."

"Is that an invitation for breakfast?" he wiggled his eyebrows.

If she'd blasted him with one of her cool blue stares,

it would've been easier to laugh it off as a joke. But her pretty blush meant that she understood exactly what he had meant. "Not if you still smell like that in morning."

Despite the stench of smoke coming off him, Isaac leaned in so that their faces were so close, the soot smeared across his cheekbone could almost float over to hers. "You have a shower at your cabin, don't you?"

He heard the breath catch in her throat and felt the heat of her skin as her blush deepened. She stumbled as she took a step backward and brushed his hand away as he reached out to steady her.

Jerking her head around to peek at the doorway to the dining room, her voice was shaky when she replied, "I also have a son at my cabin."

Yes, she had a son now. Hannah would do well to remember that fact herself the next time she got a little flirtatious with a man. And not just any man, but Isaac. The person she'd thought she'd known better than anyone else in the world at one time. The person who'd once made her laugh and made her dream and made her think that there was something other than good causes that she could dedicate her life to.

But they weren't the same people anymore. Too bad her desire for him hadn't gotten the memo.

Dinner with the entire B Crew at the station that night consisted of four firefighters (including the chief), one senior volunteer (Scooter'd had to go home to find a replacement battery for his hearing aid), two paramedics, one excited little boy and one schoolteacher who was a complete nervous wreck every time the chief looked down the table at her.

His earlier touch had reminded her of their slow dance at the VFW hall, and that brought back memories of every verbal and physical exchange they'd shared in the past few weeks, which had begun blending in with her recollections of their high school summers. Her attraction to him back then had snowballed the same way, although now that Hannah was older—and had a lot more than just her reputation to lose—it was feeling less like a growing snowball and more like an avalanche.

"I still don't understand why they don't have a dog at the fire station," Sammy said later that week when they were driving down the mountain to donate some old blankets to the animal shelter outside of Boise. "Aren't they supposed to have one of those dogs with the spots on them?"

"That's just a myth," Hannah said, then saw her son's confusion in the rearview mirror. "A myth is like a legend or a story that gets told so often, people believe it."

"So we don't have to pick out a dalmatian? We could get Chief Isaac any dog we want?"

"What? No. People shouldn't pick out pets for others. If Chief Jones wants a dog, he can go get one himself."

"Oh, look," Sammy said, the lining of his coat making a rustling sound against the seat belt. "Maybe he's getting one right now."

"Huh?" But when Hannah turned into the parking lot at the animal shelter she saw the red pickup truck pulling in behind her, the gold letters with the official Sugar Falls crest stamped on its doors.

It was the chief's vehicle, the one Isaac used around town on official business when he wasn't responding to actual calls. The gravel crunched under the four-by-four's tires as he parked beside them, not making Hannah's nerves feel any steadier than they had after that unrelaxing dinner with his crew a few nights ago. Hannah leaned into the back seat to grab a stack of folded fleece, not wanting to face Isaac until her pulse slowed.

"Are you here to pick out a new dog for the fire station?" Sammy asked Isaac as soon as his driver's side door opened.

"A dog? No way. That's way too much responsibility and we're already understaffed right now with our regular workload. We don't need to add training a dog to anyone's list of duties."

"I could come take care of him," her son offered as he climbed out of the car, and Hannah's head whipped around. "Or her, if you get a girl dog."

Oh, geez. Hannah needed to put the brakes on this conversation. And she needed to do it ten minutes ago.

"If you're not here for a dog—" she asked Isaac, sending a pointed look at Sammy "—which is a very, very big responsibility, by the way, then what are you doing here?"

"I'm dropping off some blankets and thought I'd check their collection bin to see if there were any more canned goods."

"That's what we're doing." Sammy smiled.

"Yeah," Hannah seconded. "That's exactly what we were doing because this location was on my route."

"Well…" Isaac lifted his shoulders. "We'll give them double the blankets and you can be responsible for taking all the food back to Mrs. Johnston."

Hannah opened her mouth and was about to agree until she thought better of it. "Actually, it's probably best if *you* take all the food to her. She's been asking me to head up a bake sale to pay for the new teen room in the library and I've been trying to avoid her."

"Apparently, she isn't familiar with your lack of skills in the kitchen," Isaac said, the hint of a joke lifting the corners of his mouth.

"Hmph," Hannah huffed, although he had her there.

"It's not like I need to know how to bake in order to sell everybody else's baked goods."

"Can we play with some of the dogs while we're here?" Sammy interrupted, something he'd never done before. Hannah would've corrected him if it hadn't been such a normal six-year-old thing for the otherwise shy boy to do and she hadn't been working on getting him to come out of his shell more often. But she wanted to discourage Isaac from the familiar direction their banter was now taking.

"Sure," Isaac said, before seeing Hannah's disapproving expression. "I mean, we can if it's okay with your mom."

Hannah sucked in her cheeks at the man's presumptuousness, but ended up allowing Isaac—who wasn't loaded down with as many old, used blankets as they were—hold the door for her and Sammy.

The strong smell of pine cleaner, litter boxes and wet dog assaulted her nose when they walked inside.

"Here, let me help you with some of those," Isaac said, trying to grab the stack under her right arm. The backs of his fingers brushed the tender spot below her ribcage and a shot of electricity blasted through her. Instinct had her yanking her elbow inward to protect herself from the startling but sensual touch.

Unfortunately, her clampdown also pinned his hand between the blankets and her waist. He was close enough that she could see each individual lash as he lowered his eyes in a sleepy, seductive way and then smirked. "If you don't want me to help, you could just say no thanks. You don't have to trap my arm."

Hannah's wrist shot upward releasing Isaac's hand and the stack of blankets, which he effortlessly caught, damn him. She took a couple of steps to the side and tried to look down her nose at him. "Fine, but don't try to take credit for my donation."

"Are you guys coming?" Sammy called from the oblong reception desk where a man with a thick shock of gray hair and a matching beard down to his chest sat manning a clipboard. If he hadn't been wearing khaki pants and a green polo shirt with a volunteer nametag that identified him as Frank, the gentleman might've been mistaken for Santa Claus.

"Just what we needed before the winter," Frank told them when they relinquished the blankets. Hannah felt like she should recognize the gentleman, but the animal shelter was closer to Boise than it was to Sugar Falls and it was more likely that its volunteers lived in the city.

Hannah smiled. The feeling of doing some good for someone else, even a four-legged animal, never failed to lighten her heart with a joyful satisfaction. "Chief Jones is also here to pick up any canned goods people might've left for the Sugar Falls food drive."

She felt the heat of Isaac's stare on the right side of her face and knew that if she so much as glanced in his direction, she'd see Isaac giving her an *Oh, really?* look. But Hannah didn't care. She needed to get him to take the canned food items and go before anyone—especially her son—noticed the way her body kept reacting every time Isaac got too near.

"And we're also here to play with some dogs," Sammy added, again pleasing Hannah with the realization that he was starting to find his own voice and growing comfortable talking in front of strangers.

Hannah nodded toward where someone had painted a sign that said Kitty Korral. She whispered to her son, "Go ahead and take a peek at the new kittens. I'll meet you over there in a second."

Sammy didn't have to be told twice before he was darting to the large window on the back wall. Hannah squared her shoulders, then thought better of it and attempted a more casual pose before speaking to Isaac. "So, uh, thanks for taking the food back to Sugar Falls. I better catch up with Sammy before he falls in love with all the animals."

"Fine," Isaac said. "But when I drop them off with Mae Johnston, I'll let her know that you're planning to take the lead on making all the cupcakes for the library bake sale, too."

Hannah's ears burned at the reference to when she was sixteen, going through her vegan phase and had tried to make her now-infamous silken tofu mini bundt cakes for the Christmas in July craft bazaar. She hadn't taken into account how crumbly they would be, and the bold squirrels in Town Square Park had darted across the grass, over pedestrians and picnic blankets, scaring city folks and some children as they filled their tiny cheeks with all the fallen pieces.

"If you tell her that, then I'll tell Freckles and Cessy Walker that you came up with a brilliant idea to do a sexy firefighter calendar to raise funds to build a new gazebo in Town Square Park."

Instead of shocking him into silence, Hannah's words made Isaac chuckle. "They tried to do that last year and I already told them in no uncertain terms that it would never happen. But it's nice to know that you've also been giving some thought to seeing racy photos of me."

Hannah gasped. "You wish," she told him, but that was exactly what she'd been thinking, blast his self-satisfied smile.

If she'd dared a glance below Isaac's neck, she wouldn't have been surprised to see his hands rubbing together in villainous glee—as though he had her right where he wanted her.

"Well, if the rest of the fire department looks like this one—" Frank gave Isaac a bold, appraising look "—I could unload a coupla dozen of those calendars for you."

Sucking in her cheeks, Hannah swallowed her chagrin at forgetting that there was another person there, witnessing her attraction to Isaac.

"Thanks," Isaac told Frank, then he looked around the lobby. "Did someone move the collection box?"

"Oh, yes. Forgot to mention that earlier." Frank used his thumb to gesture toward a dry-cleaning bag hanging from a handle on one of the filing cabinets. "Mae Johnston stopped by this morning to drop off my red suit. She's my Mrs. Claus when we do the Santa visit to the children's hospital. But that's not who the calendars would be for, mind you. We also do the North Pole Poker Run for my motorcycle club."

"Hmm." Isaac tilted his head. "I guess I could see Mae as Mrs. Claus. She has the right hair for it, even if she's not exactly the sweet, grandmotherly type. I could definitely see her at a biker rally, though."

Hannah's fingernails dug into her palms. What did Mae Johnston and Santa suits and biker rallies have to do with anything? And why wasn't Isaac in any hurry to correct the assumption that he wasn't actually going to pose for a sexy firefighter calendar? At least, she hoped that was a misconception. Either way, she couldn't keep the frustration from her voice as she pointedly asked, "So, about that food collection box?"

"Mae picked up the box when she dropped off the suit," Frank said slowly, as though he'd mentioned that when they first walked in, which he obviously hadn't. Otherwise Hannah would've already been on her way.

"Okay, well, now that we've got all of that clear," she said, rolling back on her boot heels, "I'll leave you two to talk about…whatever…and I'll just go catch up with Sammy and take him to play with the dogs."

"Make sure you check out the new litter of puppies that came in yesterday," Frank called out. "They're adorable and you could use them when you do your hunky fireman calendar."

Hannah blew out a sigh, fighting the urge to turn around and tell Frank that there wasn't going to be a stupid calendar.

"Thanks, man. We'll let you know." Isaac's voice was way too close and that *did* cause Hannah to turn around right before she got to where her son had his face pressed up against the kitten nursery viewing window.

"Why are you still here?" she whispered to Isaac out of the side of her mouth.

"Because I told Sammy we could look at dogs." He opened the door that led toward the animal kennels and the boy dashed through. Looking back at Hannah, he extended his arm as though he was ushering her inside. "You coming with us or did you want to hang out here with Frank and talk about which poses you think I should do for my upcoming photo shoot?"

Hannah's back molars unclenched long enough for her to grumble, "The only pose I'm interested in seeing is the one where you're walking out the exit door."

Isaac winked at her as she marched past him to follow her son. His voice was low and smooth and directly behind her ear when he caught up to her angry stride. "You always did like the view of my butt."

Chapter Ten

"She kinda looks like a dalmatian," Sammy said to Isaac, and Hannah had to bite her lip to keep from correcting the boy. After all, it wasn't her child's fault that Isaac had barged in uninvited on their visit to the animal shelter, getting her all flustered and then putting her on the defensive.

"Well, she's white with some black markings," Isaac replied as he gently removed a set of tiny canine incisors from the laces of his boot and urged the spotted puppy back toward her solid-colored siblings. He and Sammy sat on the concrete floor and rolled a tennis ball back and forth to each other as the four littermates gave chase, a flurry of oversize paws and wagging tails scrambling to be the first to catch the green felt orb. "But dalmatians have short hair and this girl is gonna be a total fur ball. Plus, the vet tech said they think she's part husky and part Great Dane. She's going to end up being almost twice the size of a dalmatian, aren't you, Big Dot?"

"Big Dot!" Sammy repeated and giggled so hard he fell onto his side. Hannah wanted to warn him to watch the little yellow puddle one of the pups had made when it got too excited from a vigorous belly rub a few minutes ago. But Isaac had already teased her about being a germophobe when she'd insisted on a squirt of antibacterial gel every time any of them so much as looked at a different kennel. So, instead, she stood up and went in search of some paper towels or disinfecting wipes to clean up the mess.

"I think she likes me, Mama." The sound of Sammy's belly laugh as Big Dot tried to balance on top of the six-year-old's chest made Hannah's heart stretch so much, she doubted her ribcage could contain it. Just when she thought she might burst with happiness, her son said those four little words that would force her to into the role of meanest mother in the world. "Can we keep her?"

Sighing, she sat down cross-legged beside Sammy and stroked his head, her forefinger tracing the line where his hair met his face. "I don't think that would be a good idea, sweetie."

Sammy's shoulders slumped against the ground as he looked up at the ceiling, sadness filling his solemn brown eyes. The puppy wiggled its bottom and the boy absently petted her, then rolled his head so he was looking at Hannah. "Remember when we had to draw our family in class?"

Hannah's throat clogged at the memory. She'd seen the pictures hanging up in the kindergarten room when she was at the school for parent–teacher conferences the previous week, and Sammy's had been the only one with just two people in it. And those two people didn't look anything alike. She made another mental note to talk to

Choogie Nguyen's mothers as she slowly nodded at her son, waiting for the inevitable.

"Well, almost everyone had a pet in their drawing, except for me."

She let out the breath she'd been holding. Okay, so his observation could've been a lot worse. If Sammy thought an animal—and not a father, for example—was the only thing missing from his life, then maybe he was adjusting all right, after all.

She looked at Isaac, needing reassurance that she was making the right decision; however, all he did was shrug.

"But if I had Big Dot, I could ask Mrs. Kamil to take down my drawing and then I could color a puppy on it."

"Oh, sweetie," was all Hannah could say. She'd been around children all of her life, but it was different when you were raising your own child. And it wasn't like she'd had Sammy since he was a baby, giving herself time to grow as a parent along with him. He'd been four years old when she met him and under the charge of several adults who worked at the children's home. A year later, she'd started the adoption process and six months after that, he'd moved into her small cottage near the dormitory and she became his sole caretaker. Even though they'd had an instant emotional bond from the first day she'd started teaching at the orphanage in Ghana, they'd really only lived together the past several months and were still learning how to adjust to their new roles in each other's lives. She'd read countless books and articles, prepping herself for tricky parenting moments like these, but now all she could do was sit here and murmur platitudes while stroking his hair.

Hannah wanted to do better than that.

"If you take her home, Big Dot might miss all of her

brothers and sisters," Isaac offered, probably out of pity for both her and Sammy.

"When Mama brought me here, I only missed some of the kids from the home, but I don't really remember them anymore."

Hannah stifled her cry by putting her fist to her mouth. It had only been several weeks, yet already Sammy was forgetting things about the first few years of his life. She'd read that it was normal for this to happen, but reading it and feeling it were two different things.

Before she could think of what to say, Sammy scooted his entire body ninety degrees so that he could still lie down, but look at Isaac. The small dog stayed on his chest. "Do you ever miss your brothers and sisters, Chief Isaac?"

"I don't have any siblings," Isaac replied. "I was an only child."

"I don't have any, either. But Big Dot and me could be like brother and sister. Then I wouldn't be an only child."

"Sometimes being an only child can be fun," Isaac said, but Hannah knew that he didn't mean it. When they were eighteen, Isaac had told her that he'd always been lonely growing up. Of course, his parents were so absorbed in their own lives that they'd dumped their son at his Uncle Jonesy's house every summer, which wasn't quite the same situation as Sammy's.

"You might not have any siblings, but you have cousins." That was the best Hannah could do.

"Yeah," Sammy conceded cautiously, as though he wasn't fully convinced that an extended family was a suitable substitution for a dog. But at least he now had his head propped up on his elbow. "My boy cousins are fun because they're older, but my girl cousins are boring. And they still wear diapers."

"Well, you're already better off than me," Isaac said in a conspiratorial tone, as though he was confiding in the child. "I didn't have any cousins at all. Just Uncle Jonesy."

Hannah needed to stop wallowing in her sea of emotions and put a positive spin on things before this conversation got any more depressing. "You have uncles and aunts, too, Sammy. And what about Grammie and Pop Pop?"

The boy's frown didn't disappear and she hated that she sounded as though she was trying to sell the idea of family to the boy.

"I like Pop Pop, okay. But..." His voice trailed off and Hannah's stomach sank. She'd noticed the way Sammy stayed behind her whenever they went to visit her parents, and how he almost never spoke with her mom, no matter how many times Donna Gregson tried to relate to him. Hannah had rationalized it by telling herself that he'd only known them a little over a month and she'd assumed that Sammy was being his shy self. However, he didn't act the same way when it was just her father.

"Do you not like Grammie?" she asked.

Sammy sat up and looked at Isaac, then at Big Dot, who'd tumbled to his lap, then back to Isaac.

"Sweetie." Hannah put a hand on his shoulder. "Remember what I told you before we got on the airplane to come here? You can always tell me how you're feeling. Even if you think it will make me sad or mad."

"It's not that I don't like Grammie. It's just that she's sick." The boy's eyes looked toward Isaac. "Like my mother."

"You're sick?" Isaac's attention shot over to Hannah, but she didn't have the mental fortitude to address his concerns, as well. She was still reeling from the emotional minefield she'd just inadvertently exposed.

But Sammy shook his head. "Not her. She's my mama. I mean my bia…bio…" He looked at her. "What's it called, again?"

"Your biological mom?" Hannah asked and Sammy nodded. "Oh, sweetie, Grammie has a different kind of sickness."

"So she's not gonna die like my mother did?"

Hannah swallowed several times and had to look up to keep her tears from spilling over onto her cheeks. The truth was, she didn't know what her mom's long-term prognosis was. And she certainly didn't know how to explain it to a boy who'd already lost so much.

So when Big Dot let out a loud bark, Hannah said what any worn-down mother would do in that situation. "How about we find out how to take Big Dot home with us?"

She was rewarded with a shining smile from her son— but inside, she couldn't shake the fear that had haunted her ever since she'd learned of her mother's diagnosis. And when she lifted her gaze, she caught Isaac staring right at her—and knew he'd figured her out.

After having already intruded on one intensely intimate family moment at the animal rescue, Isaac spent Thanksgiving week debating whether he should further complicate things with Hannah by attending her brother's wedding this weekend. Yet every time he convinced himself to stay far away from her, Luke's words would replay in his head.

They both needed to put this thing behind them once and for all. Officially.

Unfortunately, Isaac was still second-guessing his decision to come when Kylie Gregson, Hannah's other sister-in-law, cornered him at the reception after the long-anticipated dulce de leche wedding cake had been served. "Just like that, she caved and got the dog?"

"Pretty much," Isaac replied, the condensation from his glass of whiskey and Coke making his palms wet. Or maybe it was the DJ inviting couples out to the dance floor that had him so anxious. For the hundredth time tonight, he told himself that he never should have come all the way to Twin Falls.

But he'd worked a double shift on Thanksgiving and the day after so that his employees with kids could be with their families. Isaac had needed the break away from town. He'd thought it'd be simple enough to disappear in the crowd, since the wedding's resort location was packed with almost everyone from Sugar Falls, along with at least a third of the population of Carmen's hometown of Las Vegas. But everyone related to Hannah—either by blood or marriage—had tracked him down, going out of their way to talk to him.

But it was Kylie who put him on edge with her blatant curiosity and her less-than-subtle line of questioning. "So, a few days ago, when you just happened to run into Hannah at the animal shelter, you didn't team up with Sammy to talk her into getting a puppy?"

"Me? I was right there with her, trying to reason with Sammy about the responsibility of caring for a dog," he argued, not adding that his own heart had turned to mush when the kid brought up his lack of siblings and his family portrait at school. Isaac knew all too well the feeling of missing out on something that everyone else around you seemed to have. But for good measure, he added, "Besides, how could I talk Hannah into anything? She hates me."

"First of all, Hannah Gregson is incapable of hating anyone. She's too noble for that." Kylie lifted a second finger. "Second of all, I didn't live in Sugar Falls during those youthful summers, but from what I hear, I probably wouldn't blame her for hating you *if* she did. Which she doesn't."

Fair enough. There had been a time long ago when Isaac hadn't cared very much for his actions, either.

"Third," Kylie continued, "I meant, did you talk her into it in one of those reverse psychology ways? Like telling them they shouldn't get a dog because you knew she would do the exact opposite just to spite you?"

While Isaac had definitely picked up on Hannah's tendency to want to do the complete opposite of whatever he suggested, he'd also picked up on the fact that Sammy might need something that made the child feel as though he belonged, as though he was needed. Looking back on the conversation now, Isaac might've taken a different approach and suggested that being the dog's caretaker would actually give Sammy a role in his new household, a sense of purpose.

However, the Gregson household, along with the people in it, really shouldn't concern him at all. His tone still sounded defensive, though, when he replied, "How would it spite me? It's none of my business whether she gets a pet or not."

"And fourth," Kylie continued, apparently not done yet, "have you two ever thought about just sitting down and having an actual conversation about the fact that you're both still crazy for each other? I can tell you from firsthand experience that it really would do wonders for your relationship."

Isaac barely caught the cocktail glass before it slipped out of his hand and shattered on the ground. "What did you say?"

"I said I know from firsthand experience—"

"Not that part." He circled his finger in a loop as

though he could rewind her words. "I mean the part about both of us still being crazy for each other."

Kylie's eyes shot upward before she huffed and muttered something about idiotic men. But he couldn't ask her for any more clarification because Hannah chose that moment to walk up to them, her pale pink bridesmaid's dress tailored perfectly to her figure.

Isaac lifted his drink to his lips and tried to look busy.

"Mom is tiring out already." Hannah spoke quietly to her sister-in-law. "But she's insisting that all of the grandkids hang out in the motor home with her and Dad now that it's past their bedtime. I know that was the original plan, but I don't want her wearing herself out."

"Is that their motor home out front?" Isaac asked. He'd noticed that it was parked awfully close to the red-painted curb, and the first responder in him had gone out of his way to make sure there was alternate access for a fire engine to park, in the event one was needed. He had a habit of doing that no matter where he went, even if he was at some huge resort hotel two hours south of his jurisdiction.

"Yes. We tried to get them to stay in one of the rooms, but my mom said the hotel would be too busy with it being a holiday weekend and she'd be more comfortable having her own bed and stuff nearby."

"Hannah." Kylie draped an arm loosely around her sister-in-law's shoulder. "I think that if your mom is insisting and your dad is going to be with her, then let them spend some time with their grandchildren. It's important to her, and the kids love hanging out in their RV. We're only a few hundred yards away and can take turns going out there and checking on them."

Hannah bit her lower lip. "Okay, but maybe only for an hour or so?"

"My girls are gonna fall asleep on the walk out there."

Kylie nodded toward a double stroller holding identical twins with matching floral wreaths falling out of their hair. "Drew and I planned to take them upstairs to our room afterward, anyway. Don't worry, okay?"

"It's hard not to." Hannah's admission caught Isaac by surprise. She usually acted as though she was more than capable of handling anything under the sun. It had him wondering if her hesitation now had something to do with Sammy's recent revelation and concerns about his adoptive grandmother.

"Then let me distract you." Kylie handed Hannah her flute of champagne. "Speaking of kids—and now a dog—hanging out in RVs, I was just talking to Isaac here about how you always swore you weren't a dog person, but then you caved and got Sammy a new puppy."

"Isaac told you that, did he?" Hannah squinted one eye at him before she took a large swig of champagne.

He held up his palm. "I didn't tell her anything she didn't already know."

"Oh, you two with your constant defensiveness." Kylie snagged a second glass from a passing server and traded it out with the empty one in Hannah's hand. "I've said it before and I'll say it again. What you both need is a couple of drinks, a slow dance and a long make-out session."

"Ugh, Kylie!" Hannah wrinkled up her nose. "Please don't tell me about your firsthand experience again. I don't want to think of my brother Drew doing any of that."

Isaac fought back a grin, experiencing some relief that she'd gotten the same lecture he had. And a little more relief that Hannah's first response hadn't been abject horror over doing those things with him.

Kylie wiggled her eyebrows. "Maybe you should do less thinking and more kissing and making up?"

Hannah gasped as her sister-in-law gave her a little hip check before sauntering away, causing Hannah to side-step in her high heels. Isaac reached out to steady her, grabbing one side of Hannah's waist. Feeling the heat of her skin under the gauzy fabric, he suddenly wondered if maybe he was the one who needed to be steadied.

"I hope you know she doesn't mean it." Hannah's voice was so strained, he had to dip his head lower to hear her over the Bruno Mars song blasting from the dance floor.

"Mean what?" Isaac knew exactly what Hannah was talking about, but he wanted to hear her say it. He wanted to know if such a thing was even an option with them.

"What she said about us making up," Hannah whispered. The flush stealing up her cheeks suggested that, although she didn't repeat it, she was definitely thinking about the kissing part of the equation. "Especially since people are now starting to look this way. I should probably go check on…um…something."

Her eyes darted around the room, but it was clear that there was nothing left for her to do tonight but relax and enjoy herself.

"I think Kylie's right," he told her, pulling her free hand into the crook of his arm. "You definitely need a distraction."

Chapter Eleven

Hannah would've protested if Isaac had tried to lead her onto the dance floor at that exact moment. So it was a good thing he'd suggested taking a walk outside the ballroom, instead. On their way, they stopped at the bar in the lounge and she hung back while he ordered her another drink. Coming out, they saw that one of the small seating areas near the grand fireplace in the lobby was empty and, without much discussion, she soon found herself sinking into one of the velvet-upholstered club chairs opposite him.

With the cozy fire, the dim lighting and the small flickering candle on the low table between them, the scene was way too intimate for Hannah's liking. Especially with Kylie's words about needing a long make-out session still echoing in her ears. However, she also didn't want it to seem like she was purposely avoiding him because that would only reinforce the awkwardness between them. She might as well get used to making small talk with the guy because, clearly, neither one of them was going anywhere.

"I can't believe this place already has all their holiday decorations up," Isaac said, taking the lead on the small talk as he nodded toward the fifteen-foot Christmas tree separating the lobby from the hotel's registration desk. Fresh evergreen wreaths with red velvet bows were evenly spaced out just above the dark mahogany wainscoting along the walls, and a brass menorah stood proudly in the center of a display table under the wide window near the entrance, still waiting for its candles.

"Sammy said the same thing when we checked in on Wednesday."

"So, then, did you have Thanksgiving dinner here?" he asked.

"Yeah. With all the wedding preparations going on, nobody in my family really wanted to cook. What about you and Jonesy? Did you guys do anything special?"

"I was on duty and the crew did a potluck at the station and invited a few of the local seniors who didn't have anywhere else to go. Somehow, my uncle and Scooter talked Freckles into making her famous biscuits and a couple of sweet potato pies." At this rate, they were going to be discussing their favorite stuffing recipes next. Isaac must've sensed the same thing because he leaned closer and rested his forearms on his knees. "Hannah, listen. I don't know what's going on between us. And, as much as you like to act as if you're in control, I'm getting the feeling that you aren't really sure, either. So maybe we should stop beating around the bush and just say whatever we feel and see where things take us."

That was the problem. Hannah knew from experience where things would take them if she wasn't careful. And she wasn't quite sure that was a path she should go down again.

Sighing, she massaged her temples before diving in headfirst. "Just so you know, I don't always get into heavy conversations with my son in front of puppies and strangers."

"I'm not exactly a stranger, though, am I?" Isaac asked. His knowing stare and the strong outline of his chiseled jaw when he smiled weren't making things any less intimate.

Hannah shivered, then shifted in her seat. "It's just that I didn't realize that Sammy was going to bring up his biological mother or my mom like that, and it was kind of an intense family conversation that he and I probably should've had in private."

"You do that a lot."

"Do what a lot?"

"Like to have conversations in private. Or not even have them at all." He held up his palm when she leaned forward defensively. "Relax. I'm not bringing up the past. I'm just pointing out that you don't like confrontation about your personal business. It's nothing to be ashamed of. You like peace and harmony and for everybody to be happy. It can be quite endearing, actually."

"Careful, Isaac, or it might sound like you're trying to give me a compliment."

He rolled his eyes. "My point is that it's okay for you to let your guard down in front of other people. Even me. The kid was being honest with his feelings and you don't want to teach him to stifle those."

He was right. She shouldn't be ashamed that her son was straightforward about how he felt. As a mother, she wanted that for her child. It was just the bad timing of the whole thing. Hannah sank back into her chair, letting the heat from the fireplace lure her into a warm reprieve.

"Would it be incredibly nosy to ask you how his mom died?" Isaac's eyes were sympathetic and his mouth formed a soft line of concern. Hannah knew that he was being sincere and not just looking for juicy details like many of the other people who'd asked the same question.

"He was an infant. She was only fifteen and was also an orphan at the children's home. Nobody even knew the girl was pregnant until the night she gave birth."

"How terrifying that must have been for her," Isaac responded.

"I know. The director told me that the lack of prenatal care was a big factor. She had preeclampsia and the spike in her blood pressure caused her brain to just shut down."

"And his father?"

"Nobody knew, since she'd recently arrived from another town and died so soon after giving birth. Normally, they don't allow international adoptions if the child still has living family, so that was one of the reasons I was able to adopt Sammy. Well, that and the fact that I established residency by living in the village when I was a teacher there."

After a long pause, Isaac lifted the corner of his mouth and said, "I can see why you would want to be his mother. Sammy is an incredible child."

Hannah swallowed the lump of emotion that clogged her throat. If she wasn't careful, her heart was going to be putty in Isaac's hands once again. She blinked back a few tears, but her voice was raw when she said, "Thank you."

"Speaking of mothers, how's yours?" he asked, probably thinking he was doing her a favor by giving her a chance to unload about her mom. He wasn't.

"She's...well, she's... I don't know what to say."

"Come on, Hannah. It's okay to talk out loud to some-one. Even to me." It was almost as if he were daring her to open up, and damn if she wasn't tired of holding it all in. Besides, she'd already discussed Sammy's family situation, why couldn't she talk about her own?

She took a sip of her champagne, the cold bubbles turning into a warm fizzle as it made its way to her tummy. "About six years ago, my mother went in for a mammogram and they found a small tumor. She had the lumpectomy and the radiation and hoped for the best. We all did. It was hard on her, but it was especially hard on my dad.

"A year and a half after that, they found the same thing, smaller this time, but in the same breast. Mastectomy, chemo, hormone treatments, she went through all of it and hated every second. It was way more intense the second time around, and really took a toll on her. But she fought hard and got through it.

"Afterward, she went into remission and got a clean bill of health at every follow-up appointment for the next couple of years. So she and my dad decided to celebrate by buying an RV and going on their dream trip, camping their way across America. I figured—we all figured—there was nothing left to worry about.

"The day they bought the motor home was the same day they bought me my plane ticket for Ghana. They knew I'd always wanted to teach abroad and that there was no way I would leave the country if there was even the slightest possibility that my mom was still sick."

"You're the ultimate caretaker, so I could see why they would think that." Isaac nodded. "Then, if she was better, what happened?"

"Then...pow." Hannah made the sound of an explosion because that's what it had felt like when her dad picked her and Sammy up at the airport her mom already wasn't feeling well enough to come meet her newest grandchild, despite the fact that Hannah had expedited the adoption process to get home sooner. "She'd been doing so well, we were all lulled into thinking that as long as her PET scan results were normal again, she was as good as cured. But now the cancer is showing up in the nearby lymph nodes."

Isaac wasn't even sure what to say. He felt awful for the Gregsons. "Man, that sucks."

"You know what? You're right." Hannah felt the emotional dam she'd erected around her heart begin to quiver. "Usually, everyone wants to apologize or ask what's going to happen or give a suggestion on what she should do, since their cousin or their neighbor or their mechanic's wife had the same thing. Sometimes, it just feels good to hear someone say what we're all thinking. It *does* suck."

A blast of party music sounded behind them as one of the ballroom doors opened up, but it was only a wedding guest—someone from Carmen's side of the family, Hannah assumed, since she didn't recognize them—heading toward the lobby exit. She and Isaac should probably get back to the reception before anyone noticed that they were both gone. But Hannah didn't feel like putting her happy-bridesmaid face back on just yet.

She felt like having some time to herself and drinking away her disappointments. She felt like being human and acknowledging her feelings, like relying on someone else for a change instead of always being the one to volunteer to fix the world's injustices. Before Sammy came into her life, she'd known that being a single mom would come with very few breaks, and she wouldn't trade that for all the vacations in the world. But since Drew had just texted her a picture of her son happily doing the Chicken Dance inside with his cousins, she pushed her guilt aside and used the few minutes she had free to finally get everything off her chest.

"The first time it happened, my mom didn't want to tell anyone." Hannah instinctively made a move to push a strand of hair off her forehead, only to realize that the hairdresser had used so much extra-firm spray, nothing had budged from the tight updo. A nervous chuckle escaped. "I guess avoiding unfortunate topics runs in my family."

Instead of laughing at her self-deprecating joke, he stood up and moved his chair the short distance across the lobby rug so that it was right next to hers. He took her hand in his own, laced their fingers together and brought it up for a kiss. But he didn't say anything. Which made Hannah more determined to keep talking, otherwise she would start thinking about how soft and warm his lips had felt on her skin.

"Anyway, it was easier for everyone in my family to not talk about it—even with each other. Well, besides my brother Drew, but he's a psychologist and was on deployment. It was right after Luke's first wife died and nobody wanted to think about the possibility of losing my mom, too. The second time, it was harder to keep quiet because everyone at my dad's church started noticing that the youth pastor's wife had been missing a lot of services. Some members thoughtfully tried to organize a dinner rotation and drop off meals for them, but my mom hated the extra attention."

"And this time?" Isaac asked.

"This time," Hannah started, but she had to choke down her sadness before she could continue. She lifted her glass to her lips for a swallow of champagne. "This time, she's just done with fighting. She refuses to go through with any more intensive treatments. We don't know how much longer she has, but the goal is to just keep her as happy and as comfortable as we can."

"Hence the reason your brother didn't want any tension between the two of us today in front of your mom."

Hannah sighed. "That's partly it."

"And the other part?"

"This afternoon, right before we took the family pictures, my dad gave me and my brothers this big speech about how important it was for my mom to see all of her children settled down with steady career paths and families of their own. You know, happy with their life choices and all that."

"And are you?"

"Am I what?"

"Settled down and happy with your life choices?"

"I think I am." His fingers were playing with hers and the sensation was doing something weird and wobbly to her insides. "I mean, of course I am. I have the job I've always wanted and a wonderful son. What more could she want for me?"

Isaac was saved from answering by the appearance of Luke opening the ballroom doors. The groom, who had to be at least fifty yards away, cupped his hands and yelled out, "Time for all the single folks to try and catch the bouquet and the garter. That's right, I'm talking to you two all cozy over there by the fireplace. Let's go!"

Hannah buried her face in her palm. It would've been less obnoxious if Luke had just paid to display the same message in the marquee lights of the Remington Theater in downtown Sugar Falls. She finally raised her eyes to Isaac. "I am not going back in there until all the ridiculous matchmaking customs are over."

"Why do you have to go in there at all?" Isaac's voice was low and smooth and caused her lady parts to forget why she was out here in the first place.

"Well, I can't very well stay in the lobby and have all the well-meaning busybodies looking for me. Plus, I should probably check on Sammy."

Hannah rose to her feet, her arches protesting the resumed torture of her high heels. Isaac cupped her elbow as they slowly made their way toward the ballroom. Very slowly. As in, a box turtle could've made it there quicker.

He had no sooner opened the door for her than a boisterous cheer erupted. Hannah instinctively stepped in front of Isaac, as though she could hide him from view, as though the party guests wouldn't already have figured out that they'd been together this whole time.

"Don't worry." Isaac's breath tickled her ear as his hands came to rest on either side of her waist. "Your secret is still safe."

It was true. Nobody had even noticed their return because everyone was too busy cheering for Monica Alvarez, who'd just caught the bouquet. Still, Hannah felt ashamed at his implication that she thought of their time together as some sort of secret, even though that was exactly how she'd just reacted. It was more about preserving her privacy.

"Hey, Chief Isaac, look." Sammy ran up to them waving a scrap of fabric in his fist and Hannah tried not to frown at the fact that her son was more excited to talk to his new hero than to her. "The garter landed right on top of one of Uncle Luke's friends. Right on his head. He wasn't even trying to catch it because he said it was the same thing as catching a dog collar. So I asked him if I could have it and Pop Pop said we can take it out to the

RV right now and give it to Big Dot. But if it's too tight on her neck, she can only use it for chewing."

Hannah rubbed at the crease forming above her nose when her father joined them. She knew she should've gotten a dog sitter instead of bringing the pup on the trip with them. "Dad, are you seriously going to let Carmen's wedding garter be used as a chew toy for my dog?"

Jerry Gregson shrugged. "It's not like Carmen needs it anymore. Come on, Sammy, let's go take the girl for a walk before bedtime."

"Have Grammie and Pop Pop call me if you need anything," she told Sammy before giving him a kiss on his forehead. Then she gave him a hug. And another kiss.

Her eyes followed her father and her son as they made their way to the lobby exit. She'd forgotten that Isaac was still propping the door to the ballroom open until he asked, "Is it his first night away from you?"

Hannah let out the breath she'd been holding and nodded as the DJ started a slow song. People were drifting toward the dance floor, but she wasn't paying much attention since she kept looking over her shoulder to see if Sammy had forgotten anything. Or needed another goodnight kiss.

"So, are we going in or going out?" Isaac asked. "Or, if you want to just stand here all night, we can ask someone to find us a doorstop so my arm can take a break."

"Sorry," she said, giving her head a little shake as she tried to focus on her options.

Cessy Walker was tugging Jonesy's arm as she pulled him onto the dance floor and Freckles lifted up a forkful of cake in a salute as she yelled from her table a few yards away. "Hey, Chief, isn't this your song?"

It was then that she recognized the song playing as the same one they'd danced to at the VFW hall a couple of weekends ago. Hannah gulped. "I think I may still need a distraction. Preferably in a place where there's a lot less people."

"Luckily, I have access to somewhere a little more private." Isaac smiled at her and Hannah's knees went limp. She'd said exactly the same words to him ten years ago. Right before she'd invited him to the small boatshed behind the Gregson cabin and given him her virginity.

Isaac couldn't believe Hannah was following him upstairs to his hotel room. Not that he was planning for anything to happen. Hell, he hadn't even kissed her yet, although he'd been thinking about doing just that since the night of the VFW dinner dance. Down in the lobby, when he'd pulled his keycard out of his pocket and asked if she wanted to go somewhere more private, he wasn't sure what his intention had been, other than to give her a few moments to get herself composed after that heavy conversation they'd shared about her mom.

They didn't speak as they walked down the hallway, the thick, plush carpeting muting their steps, making the silence all the more deafening. But he remained quiet because he didn't want to risk saying anything that would scare her away.

The tiny light above his doorknob turned green, but his hand was so unsteady it slipped on the handle and he had to insert his key all over again.

"Can I get you something else to drink?" he asked, stopping by the mini fridge.

"No, I probably shouldn't. But if you don't mind..." She braced one hand on the entry wall, balancing herself as she slid each foot out of her heels. "These things have been killing me."

Isaac's mouth went dry and he yanked out a cold bottle

of water, trying not to think about what else she could remove to make herself more comfortable. "Make yourself at home."

She walked toward him and he was slow to step aside as she passed between the dresser and the bed. The thin, floaty material of her dress brushed against the fabric of his slacks and Isaac's skin flooded with heat. Did Hannah have any idea what her closeness was doing to him?

Probably not. She'd always been the type of woman who didn't go out of her way to enhance her beauty, who didn't use her looks to get what she wanted. It was why he'd fallen for her that first summer. Not only had Hannah not been impressed with all the things Isaac's dad had bought him back then, she was the one who'd made him want to work twice as hard to prove himself worthy of everything he'd been given.

She stood in front of the open window, her back to him as she looked out at the night sky, and he walked up behind her. "You should see the view in the daytime."

"I can imagine it right now."

"You always could see things for what they really were. People for who they really were."

The light from the lamp near the desk caused a muted reflection in the glass and she didn't have to turn around to make eye contact with him. She didn't step away when he stood close to her. In fact, it could've been wishful thinking on Isaac's part, but it almost felt as though she was arching her back, leaning toward him.

Using their reflections, Isaac's eyes stayed locked on hers as he put a hand on her waist. Heat raced up his spine when she put her own palm over his and held him there. Hannah's admission downstairs had been emotional and he wasn't the type of guy who took advantage of a female when she was vulnerable—not that Hannah would ever allow herself to be vulnerable. Still, he wasn't about to put the moves on her if she wasn't willing.

As Isaac drew in a deep breath, his chest pressed against the smooth, bare skin of her back. He was aching to touch her. Hannah pulled on his hand, dragging it along her waist until it was settled onto the flat plane of her stomach. He spread his fingers, his thumb brushing the seam in the fabric just below her breasts.

"You still smell the same," he said, his voice shakier than he'd intended. "Like that pear and honey lotion you used to buy at the farmer's market."

Her head tilted back until it rested on his shoulder, putting her forehead mere inches from his lips. "Your hands still feel the same. Although I have a feeling other parts of you have changed."

"Like what?"

"Like your arms. They seem bigger." She ran her free hand up over his biceps and Isaac's muscles instinctively flexed.

"Fire hoses are very heavy."

"And your chest seems wider." Hannah turned in his arms, her fingers trailing over his pecs to the knot in his tie. She eased it loose and Isaac gulped, keeping both of his palms planted steadily on her hips.

Hannah undid the first few buttons of his shirt, her thumbs tracing along his velvety dark skin as she made her way down. He threw back his head and groaned before pulling her hips closer against his own, the length of his erection pressed against her.

"I see that hasn't changed," she whispered as she reached between their bodies to unbuckle his belt.

Her eyes were steady as she stared into his, not needing to watch what she was doing because it was all by feel. By the time her fingers landed on his zipper, his hand was cupped along the back of her head, and he lowered his face and claimed her lips in a searing kiss.

Or, rather, she claimed his.

He would've liked to take his time, to savor every second, every touch. But Isaac had waited too long for this moment. He didn't know where his moans ended and hers began, but they both worked frantically to remove every item of clothing between them. He caught a glimpse of her bare backside reflected in the window, but before he could study and admire those curves, she was stepping forward, moving him toward the bed.

"Are you sure this is what you want, Hannah?" he asked when the backs of his knees hit the mattress and he went down onto the bed. He leaned on his elbows, watching her as her eyes seemed to drink in the length of him. Isaac had asked her the same question ten years ago, and just like then, he held his breath, waiting for her response.

Like then, she answered by slowly unpinning her hair. But that was where the similarities stopped. Because, this time, they were older, they were wiser and they had years of pent-up desire to make up for.

Their bodies came together in a clash of heat, their hands touching everywhere their mouths couldn't. Hannah straddled him, rocking her hips as she slid herself against his shaft. It would only be a matter of seconds before he slipped inside and it took every ounce of strength to hold her still.

"I need to get something," he whispered before reaching toward the floor, feeling around for his pants. Finally, his hand landed on them and he was able to retrieve his wallet out of the pocket.

"I'm glad to see you brought your own," she said, referring to that night in her boatshed when she'd had to pull a box of condoms out of the drugstore bag she'd hidden under a life vest.

"In my defense, I didn't exactly know what you had planned."

"I didn't, either." Hannah's nipples were tight and hard, pressing against his side as she watched him unroll the condom. "I still don't."

Then she raised herself over him again before gently lowering her body on his. After that, she proceeded to show Isaac that all of the planning in the world couldn't have prepared him for how incredible it would feel when they finally came back together.

Chapter Twelve

A humming sound penetrated Hannah's fuzzy brain. She opened her eyes to pitch blackness and kept absolutely still as her mind tried to orient itself. Her body was warm, her limbs relaxed, despite the heavy weight across her stomach. What was that? Tentatively reaching down, she sucked in a deep breath when she encountered the steely forearm draped over her waist.

Isaac.

She was in his hotel room. More importantly, she was completely naked in his hotel room, pressed up to him in the huge king-size bed. She hadn't had so much to drink that she'd forgotten what they'd done when she followed him up here the previous night. And she hadn't had so much that she'd forgotten the first time they'd made love, ten years ago, either. Not that she had been comparing the two experiences, but back then it had been sweet, slightly clumsy and so very poignant.

Last night had been anything but. It was as if all that time apart had built up between them and they'd finally come together in a clash of passion and intensity. And if Hannah was being honest with herself, their connection was even more powerful now, her climax had been more earth-shattering.

There was that humming sound again. Hannah turned to the vibration coming from the glass-topped nightstand and stretched to grab her cell phone, carefully dislodging Isaac's arm without waking him. Her heart sped up when she saw the notification of a text from her mom. It was almost two in the morning and the message was only a few minutes old.

Sammy had a bad dream and is asking for you. I'd bring him to you, but I forgot which room you're in.

Since she wasn't currently in her own, she should've felt relief that her mom had forgotten. That her mom and Sammy weren't standing on the other side of the door to room 406, wondering where she was. Instead, the only thing she felt was a sharp stab of shame for abandoning her son when he needed her, leaving the boy with her mother while Hannah played a game of rekindle the romance with her former flame.

Whipping her head around, Hannah used the dim light of her screen to confirm that Isaac was still asleep. It was bad enough that she'd fallen under his spell so easily last night. She didn't need him seeing her in the light of day to remind her of what an easy conquest she'd been. Again.

That wasn't fair. If anything, Isaac had been the hesitant one and Hannah had been the one to make the first... No. She needed to get out of here, not relive the way her body had come alive just from the way he looked at her.

She sat up gently; it seemed to take forever to scoot off the bed without shaking him awake. Now, what had she done with her dress? Rather, where had she been standing when she'd willingly and shamelessly taken it off? She hit her big toe on the wooden leg of the high-backed chair in the sitting area, dropping her phone and muffling a yelp. Hannah sank to her knees and patted the carpet around her as she blindly searched for her cell.

When she finally found it, she used the flashlight app to hunt for her lost clothing, but had to keep the thing angled downward so she didn't accidentally shine it in Isaac's direction. Finding the blush chiffon dress piled in a heap near the edge of the sofa was relatively simple, and when Isaac let out a mild snore and rolled onto his back, a pair of nude panties tumbled off the bed. But after several more seconds of searching, Hannah decided that she would just have to live without her strapless bra.

Still kneeling on the floor, she shimmied into her dress and got a kink in her neck twisting to zip up the back. She stood and padded in her bare feet back to the nightstand to retrieve her little purse, then remembered that she'd taken her heels off as soon as they'd arrived. Hannah scooped those up on her way out, the straps hanging from her thumb as she tried to balance her phone and purse in one hand as she used the other to ease the door closed.

An adrenaline-fueled rush of air tore out of her lungs and she looked at the mirror in the hallway, her chest rising and falling as she tried to congratulate herself for escaping unnoticed. However, the only thing she could tell her reflection was that there was no way she could go collect her son wearing a rumpled dress and the shoes that had been pinching her feet all night. It didn't help that all the bobby pins from her updo were long gone, while the gallon of extra-hold styling spray remained, making her resemble a vixen from an eighties rock music video.

She was supposed to be asleep. Or, at least, asleep in her own room. She couldn't very well show up on the front step of her parents' RV looking like she'd just done the walk of shame. Hannah debated how long it would take her to run up to her room so that she could change into something more appropriate. Even her pajamas would be a vast improvement and make it more believable that she'd been in bed when she'd gotten the text—her own bed.

But the vibrating phone in her hand made the decision for her. "Hi, Mom." She answered the incoming call, wishing she hadn't turned her ringer off and missed the first text. "I'm on my way to come get Sammy."

"Actually, your dad got him back to sleep so I was calling to tell you to just leave him here."

"Maybe I should still head that way?" Hannah offered in a hushed voice, looking over her shoulder as she did a tiptoe run to the elevator. "Just in case he wakes up again?"

"No. The poor guy was just a little overstimulated is all. It's been a big day with lots of excitement and the boys ate so much cake and did all that showing off on the dance floor. I got exhausted just watching them."

The reminder of her mom's health made Hannah want to insist all the more. "But you'll rest better if I bring him back to my room."

"Don't worry about me." Donna Gregson gave her classic response as Hannah stepped inside the elevator. "Besides, your dad has gone back to sleep next to Big Dot on the kitchen floor, since Sammy is on the dinette conversion bed. There's no way to get through there without waking him up, too. Let me just write down your room number, and if Sammy has another bad dream, your dad will bring him straight up to you."

Hannah told her, then disconnected and stared at the round buttons on the elevator wall. She should've just gone to the fourth floor last night, instead of getting out on three with Isaac. They could've avoided all of this. But avoiding things was what had gotten Hannah into this situation in the first place.

As the doors opened on her floor, Hannah stepped out into the quiet corridor. Now that her flight instincts had settled and she was no longer in the midst of her mad-dash escape, the tingling ache in her body grew with every step she took. Like something that had been lying dormant for so long just woke up and had a taste of what it hadn't even known it was missing. Which was true enough, she had to admit, literally and otherwise.

Unfortunately, she was going to have a hell of a time convincing her body that it didn't want more.

Isaac wiped the sweat off his face with a hand towel as he left the small gym in the joint basement below the police and fire stations on Monday morning.

It had taken every ounce of self-discipline he'd possessed to not call Hannah after he woke up alone in his hotel room on Sunday morning. When he fell asleep, sated in her arms, he'd truly believed they'd finally turned a corner. That maybe they could now put everything behind them and even possibly start again.

But she'd sneaked out while he'd slept, like the high tide taking the glowing embers from a beach bonfire out to sea, his burning hopes floating away with her. No note. No text. No explanation. She'd needed a distraction last night, and he'd provided it, but he was sure her worry about her son and her mom and her reputation had quickly returned with the light of day. It was possible that an emergency had come up with either Sammy or Donna Gregson, but why wouldn't she have woken him?

He could've hung around the hotel lobby waiting to catch a glimpse of her going to the family brunch—which he hadn't been invited to—but for all he knew she'd already returned to Sugar Falls. Besides, what would he say to her if he did see her? She was the one who held all the answers. Who held all the control.

She always had.

That was what happened when a man blindly put his heart in the hands of another. Not that he was repeating history or putting his heart out there again. Isaac hadn't liked his powerlessness back then and he wasn't about to tolerate it now. If Hannah wanted to pretend nothing had happened between them at the wedding, then he would double down and pretend even better.

Isaac stretched his arms over his head as he returned to the main floor. After a workout like that, he normally would've rewarded himself with a protein shake and a metaphorical pat on the back, enjoying the sense of accomplishment after bench pressing more than either of the rookie cops who'd also been working out. But Isaac was craving some sausage gravy and little bit of reassurance that his early departure from the reception with Hannah wasn't the source of any current gossip. The only place he'd find both of those things was at the Cowgirl Up Café.

After his shower and a brief discussion with Reina Garcia, the lead medic on duty, Isaac grabbed a fleece pullover and clipped a yellow walkie-talkie to his belt before jogging across Snowflake Boulevard on his way to the café. With Thanksgiving week now over, Sugar Falls wasn't even being subtle in its transformation into a winter wonderland. Of course, it helped that they'd had their first dusting of snow last night.

The public works department had gone through and hung green wreaths on every Victorian lamppost. Garlands studded with red bows and white twinkling lights were strung across each intersection. The Ski Potato Festival was scheduled for this weekend and then the holiday merriment would really kick into gear.

He kept his eyes on the lookout for Hannah's environmentally friendly compact car and felt the walls of his chest loosen when he didn't recognize any of the few vehicles parked on that block.

Isaac did, however, note his uncle's horse tethered to the hitching post right next to Blossom, Scooter's mare. The warm, sausage-scented air greeted him as he crossed the threshold of the café. This early on a Monday after a holiday weekend all but guaranteed that there would only be a handful of customers in the restaurant, and just as Isaac had expected, he knew most of them. Freckles had a spandex-clad hip propped up on the wooden armrest of a chair by Jonesy and Scooter's booth.

If Isaac was looking for gossip, he'd certainly come to the right place. Making his way to the trio, he waved at Monica, the town's librarian who sometimes picked up extra waitressing shifts at the Cowgirl Up. "Can I get a cup of decaf when you get a chance?"

His body had been humming since Saturday night and Isaac didn't need any extra caffeine coursing through him as he tried to act casual. As though he wasn't the slightest bit interested in what anybody knew about him and Hannah.

"Speak of the devil," Freckles said when Isaac slid into the booth beside his uncle. Isaac schooled his features and hoped no one saw the wince he held back.

"And he shall appear," Isaac joked with forced indifference when what he really wanted to say was *Whatever you heard about me, I can explain.*

"Did y'all have a good time at the wedding?" Freckles' question immediately put Isaac on edge. Who did she mean by *y'all*? She was looking directly at him, yet the way she was smacking her chewing gum made her face hard to read. Luckily, the old-timers at the table with him loved to hear themselves talk.

"I was just glad they kept their I do's short." Jonesy made a *tsking* sound. "All these kids with their outdoor ceremonies… Even with those heat lamps, I 'bout froze my tail off. At least they had some good country and western music afterward for the dancing."

"Biggest wedding I'd ever been to," Scooter added. "How many people you think Officer Carmen has in her family? Couple hundred? And that caramel cake? I'll tell you what, if I was lookin' to find myself a Mrs. Deets, Carmen's Aunt Lupe would be at the top of the list."

"You crazy ol' fool." Freckles shook her head, not a single strand of peach-colored hair budging out of the teased pile on top. "Aunt Lupe only gave you an extra slice so that she wouldn't have to dance with you."

"She's got you there, Scoot." Jonesy slapped a hand on the wood table, making the silverware jump as he laughed hard enough to make the booth they were sitting in vibrate. Isaac joined in to keep the attention from being directed at him. But that didn't work for long.

"And speaking of dancin', Isaac," Freckles' electric blue eyeliner made it difficult to take her direct stare seriously. "How come you weren't out there cutting the rug on Saturday night?"

"I think everyone is well aware that I don't spend much time on dance floors." He turned away from her knowing look by reaching across the table to grab a laminated menu. As if he didn't already know the thing by heart or exactly what he planned to order.

"Everyone's well aware of that, huh?" Freckles repeated. Out of the corner of his eye, he saw the older woman fold her arms across her chest, as if she wasn't about to be diverted from her choice of topic. "If I recall, you were looking pretty comfortable out there during that slow song at the VFW dinner a coupla weeks ago."

Isaac needed to change the conversation stat. Thrusting out his chin, he asked, "How's the sausage gravy this morning?"

"Same as it always is," Freckles said in a saucy tone, a hitch in her smile. "Hot and plentiful. Just like all of you bachelors at the auction."

"You're making it sound less like a charity event and more like a display of prize stallions."

"Pfsht." The sputtering voice behind him could only belong to one person. He pivoted on the cowhide covered booth and turned to look at the woman who'd left him a little over twenty-four hours ago with no explanation. "Prize stallions? You sure think awfully high of yourself, Isaac Jones."

"Maybe I have reason to," he replied, thinking of the way she'd moaned out his name on Saturday night.

Hannah had one hand on her waist, making the wool fabric of her coat flare out at her hip. Isaac grinned at the memory of how smooth and warm her skin had felt at that exact spot. He let his gaze lazily travel down her jeans to her knee-high boots and then back up to her pretty face, which now bore the most attractive rosy blush.

"It runs in the family." His uncle put a gnarled hand on Isaac's shoulder and gave him a less-than-reassuring squeeze. "A filly could certainly do worse than my nephew here."

Isaac's stomach clenched at Jonesy's ill-timed comment. While he normally appreciated the old guy's vote of confidence, he doubted Hannah would welcome the assessment. Especially after he'd just purposely reminded her of their recent night together.

"Am I the filly in question?" She lifted both brows and Freckles shifted on the arm of her chair, looking as if she was enjoying the show.

"I thought we were making horse comparisons," Jonesy said, shrugging. "Filly was s'posed to be a compliment. They're very spirited animals, you know."

"That's true," Scooter added, then put a hand over his mouth and stage-whispered to his friend. "It's not like you called her a broodmare."

Unfortunately, Scooter's lack of hearing had a direct effect on his lack of ability to whisper, and Hannah's gasp indicated she'd clearly heard.

"Where's Sammy?" Isaac asked, wondering if something had happened to her son and that was why she'd left without an explanation.

"He's in the car with Aiden and Caden. As much as I would love listening to you old boys compare me to farm animals, I should probably get back out there before they decide to use my Prius as a go-kart."

He let out a breath. Now that he knew that the boy was fine, the next question he wanted to ask was if everything was okay between them. But it wasn't like he could bring that subject up here.

"Hey, Hannah," Monica said somewhat shyly, before handing Isaac his cup of decaf. "Did you want to place your order for the bake sale?"

"What bake sale?" Jonesy asked.

"For the library," Isaac and Hannah answered simultaneously, but it was Hannah who tilted her head at him in surprise as everyone else grew silent. They hadn't discussed the fundraiser after that day at the animal shelter, but Isaac had already bought all his ingredients and reserved a booth at the upcoming Ski Potato Festival. So if she was going to be uncomfortable working with him at the event, now was her chance to back out.

"We're, uh, raising money for the new teen area." Monica was the first to speak, her voice quiet, as though she were manning the reference desk instead of trying to defuse the tension in the coffee-scented air.

"That's right," Hannah agreed. "Monica asked me to head it up."

She was speaking to the entire table, but Isaac heard the subtle dare in her words. Did she think that he wouldn't participate if she was going to be there?

"Funny, because the mayor asked me to schedule the shifts for the volunteers manning the booth." Isaac's hairline rose as he offered the challenge. He would force Hannah to talk about their night together, even if he had to do so while he was selling cupcakes on Saturday.

Several pairs of eyes darted back and forth as the silence stretched between them until finally Freckles threw up her arms. "Oh, you two kids need to just sleep with each other and get it over with."

Monica gasped before slowly backing away, the coffeepot clutched in front of her like a shield.

That was the second time someone had made the tongue-in-cheek suggestion. However, the joke was on Freckles and Kylie and everyone else who thought the only problem between him and Hannah was simply due to repressed sexual tension. The fact of the matter was that they'd already tried sleeping together, and instead of clearing things up between them, it had only muddied the waters.

Chapter Thirteen

The Ski Potato Festival, consisting of a parade and craft fair, was the first Saturday in December—only one week after she'd slept with Isaac. She'd seen all the questions in his eyes a few days ago at the Cowgirl Up Café, and several times since then, she'd picked up her phone, wanting to send him a text to explain that what had happened in that hotel room should never happen again. But putting it all into words would give the event entirely too much significance. She needed to maintain the pretense that she was over him, and the only way to do that was to prove it by working alongside him at the bake sale.

Walking into the enormous white tent temporarily erected in the middle of Town Square Park, Hannah balanced the bakery boxes loaded with four dozen apple-spice muffins, her steps getting faster as she saw the odd placement of the folding tables at their assigned booth.

"You brought *store-bought* items?" Isaac appeared

from behind one of the partitions, a ladder under his arm and a gray woolen beanie pulled low over his forehead. The knitted wool framed his hazel eyes, making them more intense, more compelling. Could he be any better looking?

Or any earlier?

How had he gotten here before her? Before anyone, really, because Hannah had purposely tried to be the first to arrive this morning to ensure that their prime selling location inside the heated tent didn't get commandeered by the local quilting club, whose reputation for craft fair booth encroachment was legendary.

"They're not from the store." She felt her defenses rising and wished she'd just swallowed her pride earlier this week and backed out of working at this stupid bake sale.

Okay, the bake sale wasn't stupid. Her heart was. Not that she'd given it a fair opportunity, but Isaac had also had plenty of chances to call or text Hannah after their night together and he hadn't. Not that she wasn't already convinced that sleeping with the man hadn't been a mistake.

Still.

It would've been nice to think that he didn't have the same regrets.

"You're saying that you just so happen to keep pink boxes at your house?" One side of his sexy lips curved up in a teasing smirk.

"My muffins are from a bakery, not a store." They'd also set her back fifty bucks—sixty if she counted the Betty Crocker mixes she'd ruined before buying these. Lifting her nose in the air, Hannah decided that she didn't have to explain her lack of culinary skills to him. Instead, she nodded toward the empty tables. "And what, exactly, did you bring?"

"My Red Hots."

"Your what?"

Isaac's chin jutted forward and his shoulders went back. "They're my famous cinnamon cupcakes with little red candies on top. They sold out at the Reclaiming the River 5K run last spring."

"Did they already sell out here, too? Because I don't see them anywhere."

She'd meant to match his teasing tone from earlier, but her words came out snarky and almost defensive. She wondered why things always had to be a battle between them. Maybe because if they were arguing, it kept them from discussing everything that needed to be said.

"They're still at the station. As you can see, I came in early to set up the booth. I guess great minds think alike."

"Well, the layout is all wrong," she said, turning to study the tables so she wouldn't have to admit that they did, indeed, think alike most of the time. And also so that she wouldn't have to remember what he looked like underneath that hooded sweatshirt with the SFFD logo stamped over his heart, right where she'd kissed his bare chest a week ago before letting her mouth travel down to his—

He lowered the aluminum ladder with a *thunk*, thankfully stopping her train of thought. "Please enlighten me with all the ways that I've messed up, oh perfect one."

The suggestion was loaded and she wasn't about to fall for it. Especially because that's what he used to say back in the day when he would tease her about all the projects she was taking on. He'd once admitted that it was the thing he'd loved most about her—her desire to save the world.

She shook her head to clear the memory. "I only meant that we should have three tables in a U-shape so that we can display the items and the volunteers can stay behind here, with the extra food."

"That's not what I was referring to, and you know it." He leaned the ladder against one of the metal poles holding up the tent. His feet were planted and his hands went comfortably into the pocket at the waist of his hoodie. He wasn't about to back down.

Hannah gulped, scanning the area for someone, anyone, who could overhear them, thereby being a justifiable excuse for keeping this intimate topic from moving forward. Damn him for being such an early riser and go-getter. Damn them both, really. They were all alone. "I have no idea what you mean. I have to go get the rest of the donated items out of my car."

But she didn't make a move to leave.

"No idea?" Isaac asked, taking a step closer to her.

Go, she commanded her feet. *Turn around and walk away.* This was no way to prove her indifference to the man. But she was rooted in place, her heart racing as Isaac closed the distance between them and she held her breath, wondering if he was going to touch her. Did it make her a hypocrite if she wanted him to?

She felt the instinctive tug of her cheek between her teeth and licked her lips to keep from appearing too nervous. Or too eager. The flick of her tongue was obviously a mistake because Isaac's eyes dipped to her mouth.

"I'm waiting," he said.

"Waiting for what?" For her?

"Waiting to hear you tell me what else I did wrong." He reached out and stroked a finger along her jawline. "Particularly last Saturday."

Hannah squeezed her eyes shut, not wanting to envision everything he'd done right that night. Her whisper came out on a soft breath. "Nothing."

"What's that?" he asked, his lips now next to hers.

"You didn't do anything wrong."

"Then why did you sneak out?"

Her lids fluttered open. "I didn't sneak out. Well, at least, not on purpose. My mom texted me that Sammy woke up from a bad dream and needed me."

"I would've gone with you to get him. Why didn't you wake me up?"

Because he's not your responsibility, she wanted to shout. Instead, she spoke with a frustrated sigh. "Because, Isaac, I don't want him taking this whole hero worship thing too far."

"But I make such a good hero. After all, I rescued you from the reception that night, didn't I?" One of his fingers traced her lower lip. Uh-oh. It wasn't just Sammy's heart she needed to protect from Isaac.

"I, uhh…" She looked at his soft mouth, thinking about all the sensual ways he'd used it on her last week.

"I didn't even get to kiss you goodbye." His low voice sent shivers down her spine.

"Did you want to?" she asked.

"I always want to."

She squeaked as his arm snaked out and wrapped around her waist, pulling her close.

Isaac had barely touched his lips to hers when the entrance to the tent flapped open with a gust of blistery wind. They jumped apart as several members of the quilting club marched inside, their arms loaded with stacks of colorful quilts and a banner that read Sugar Stitchers. It was tough to pretend that his blood wasn't pumping or that he didn't notice the way Hannah sucked in several quick, deep breaths. He told himself to be patient, that he'd get a chance to be alone with her again soon.

But soon couldn't come quickly enough. More people trickled in and the spaces filled up with other vendors displaying their crafts and wares. While they worked together silently, Isaac tried to keep his mind on the task before him instead of thinking about how good Hannah smelled every time she drifted past him as she set out the cookies and brownies and cake pops many of the townspeople had donated.

"Do you mind if I use your ladder to hang this?" Hannah asked, unrolling a long piece of butcher paper.

"Here, I can hang it." Isaac took a corner of the sign, then flinched when he saw the painted words. "Are you sure you want to put this up?"

"Oh, my gosh," Hannah clapped a hand to her mouth. "Some of my students volunteered to make the sign. It was supposed to say Bake Sale."

They both stared down at the painted words. *HOME-MADE LOVE FOR SALE.*

"I'm guessing you didn't check their work?" he said wryly.

"No. They made it in art class. It was already rolled up yesterday when the art teacher handed it to me."

He knew that her mind had picked up on the same implication by the way her eyes remained fixed on the sign. "But why?"

She didn't look at him when she responded, "Because I was busy last night writing the petition to get new funds to repave the outdoor basketball courts over by the Little League field. I didn't have time to check it."

"No, I mean why did they write this instead of Bake Sale? And, by the way, we already have the funds to redo the basketball courts. I did a recycling project in June and the kids' camp brought in aluminum cans by the bagful.

We had to wait for the permits, and then the contractors will start in the spring."

"But what about replacing the posts and backstops? They're covered with rust and—"

"Do you want to talk about some rundown basketball courts or about this?" Isaac tugged at a corner of the sign, rustling the paper to get her attention back to the subject at hand.

Hannah lifted her shoulders and dropped them. "We had this big discussion in class last week about the difference between store-bought pies and homemade pies and Elsa Folsom said that things made from scratch were made with love and worth more. Her mom is Charlotte Folsom Russell, the lady with the famous lifestyle blog who does all those cooking videos. Then Fiona Norte argued that her dad roasts all the chickens on Sundays at Duncan's Market, and just because people buy them from the store doesn't mean that Mauricio didn't cook them with love. Anyway, things got a little heated."

"Customers are lining up outside," Mae Johnston announced with a bullhorn. "We're opening up in five minutes."

Isaac felt a sense of urgency buzz through him. "Okay, I'll hang this up while you unload the rest of your muffins."

"I'm not going to stand under that sign with you," Hannah said, casting her eyes toward a woman arranging an unsteady tower of huckleberry scented candles in glass jars on the table across from them. "What will everyone think?"

Isaac rolled his eyes. "I'll be right back."

He grabbed a cinnamon roll wrapped in cellophane and jogged over to another booth. Isaac handed the local artist the treat and promised to buy one of his impressionistic paintings at the end of the day in exchange for some acrylic paint and a brush.

The main doors had been pulled back and the tourists were filtering into the tent just as Isaac stepped down from his ladder a few minutes later. Hannah bit her lip while she looked up at the changes to the banner. "I guess it'll have to do."

Isaac had squeezed in some words on top in small, purple letters. Underneath, he'd added a line, then used a blob of paint to cover up some other letters along with a few images of cookies and cakes. When he finished, the sign read, *BAKE SALE, Buy a Slice of HOMEMADE LOVE*.

"What's that brown lump supposed to be covering the last FOR SALE?" Hannah asked.

"It's a brownie."

"Hopefully, the ones we're selling end up tasting better than that one looks." Hannah moved into place behind the table and Isaac bit his tongue to keep from reminding her of the chili–spaghetti incident at the fire station.

By ten o'clock, it had become apparent that none of the other volunteers who were supposed to help with their booth were going to be relieving them any time soon. If Isaac was the suspicious type, he'd think that someone had purposely planned for him and Hannah to be stuck working the bake sale together. Alone.

Well, if they actually had been alone, it would've been fine. They could have talked about last Saturday night and possibly pick up where they'd left off—like they'd been about to do this morning before the Sugar Stitches had interrupted them. But he and Hannah weren't alone. They were in plain view of the entire town, stuck right next to each other, blocked in by the barrier of tables she'd rearranged earlier. He was trapped with her behind a wall of Officer Washington's peanut butter clusters, Mrs. Patrelli's chocolate biscotti and Principal Cromartie's banana-nut loaves.

Luckily, business was booming and they were able to avoid self-conscious closeness and a lack of conversation during the constant exchange of money for sweets. And thankfully nobody mentioned their sign, although Elaine Marconi didn't bother to stifle her giggle when she walked by.

Around eleven, Kylie Gregson maneuvered a double stroller down their aisle. Sammy trailed her with Big Dot on a leash that kept getting tangled between the excited puppy's oversize front paws. The kid's eyes lit up when he saw Isaac.

Or, at least, he wanted to believe that. As bad as it sounded to say out loud, Isaac was used to hero worship and curious attention from lots of children—it came with the job. Yet something about Sammy Gregson was different. Perhaps it was because Isaac was equally in awe of the small boy and how the child absorbed so much so quickly. In fact, Isaac usually felt lighter and more relaxed whenever Sammy was around. Most of the time, Isaac felt the need to prove he was more than just his parents' wealth. That he could make a difference in someone's life. Joining the military and then becoming a firefighter had provided him with that opportunity, but it wasn't until this very second, when he saw the affection reflected in Sammy's eyes, that he didn't feel that compulsive need to be the best.

Sammy seemed to simply appreciate him for who he was. The feeling stirred something to life inside of Isaac—a quiet contentedness he hadn't experienced since those summers with Hannah.

Not that spending the night with her again implied

that they were dating or anything, let alone forging ahead with any type of serious commitment. She was a mother now, which meant she was a package deal. If they decided to pursue anything together, their decision would ultimately affect Sammy and that was something they'd both need to consider.

Whoa. Inhaling deeply through his nostrils, Isaac commanded his brain not to get too ahead of itself here.

"People are already lining up outside for the parade," Kylie said as she set the stroller's parking brake in front of their booth. "I told Sammy we could stop by and say hi beforehand."

"Hi, sweetie," Hannah said, and Isaac envied the tender expression that crossed her face when she spoke to her son. What would it take to get her to look at Isaac that way? "Are you being good for Aunt Kylie today?"

The boy attempted to nod, but the thick fleece scarf wrapped around his neck prevented him from moving his head too much.

"Of course he is." Kylie patted Sammy's shoulder, her hand barely making a dent in the puffy down jacket. "But I left Drew outside at the hot cocoa stand with Aiden and Caden, and after that incident with the frozen marshmallows and the slingshot last year, I promised my husband we would get our candy cane cookies and come right back."

"Oooh, we sold out of those an hour ago," Isaac said, then held up two of the cupcakes he'd carefully frosted last night. "But we have a few Red Hots left."

"They look great, Isaac," Kylie started. "But I'm navigating a three-foot-wide stroller through a maze of tourists and we have to stop every twenty yards to unravel the dog, who took an unfortunate liking to the hand-carved bear on Commodore Russell's log sculpture display. So

I'm going to need something already wrapped up that I can cram into the pouch behind the seat. Oh, and some paper towels if you have them so we can go clean up the wet stump back there at the Wooden Grizzly booth."

"Thanks for adding one more to your brood today, Kylie," Hannah said as she handed over a stack of napkins. She looked at Isaac with one side of her mouth slightly quirked up. "We've been taking turns watching the boys until Luke and Carmen get back from their honeymoon."

Okay, so that was another explanation as to why she'd been too busy to get in touch with him after the wedding. Judging by the way she'd responded to his near kiss this morning, he knew it wasn't because her attraction to him had cooled.

"We better go, Sammy." Kylie unlocked the stroller and made a wide U-turn, her front wheel almost taking out Scooter Deets, who was bargaining for a lower price with the huckleberry candle vendor. The older man had his hand cupped over his ear and it would only be a matter of time before the saleslady grew tired of having to repeat herself and ended up giving him a candle for free.

"We'll save you a seat at the parade," Sammy called out over his shoulder before being tugged away by Big Dot.

Isaac lifted a hand to wave, but it froze in midair when he saw Hannah's horrified expression. He was pretty sure the last thing she wanted was to have her ex-boyfriend—and kind-of-sort-of current lover—sit with her family at the town parade.

It wasn't like it was *his* fault that her son wanted him there. If Sammy kept insisting on putting the two of them together, then Isaac couldn't very well say no, could he?

Chapter Fourteen

"It's got to be thirty degrees outside," Isaac said to Hannah over Sammy's head. "I know we're supposed to be celebrating the start of ski season, but whoever decided that having a parade in December to kick off the festivities was clearly not thinking of the Sugar Falls High School marching band."

It was bad enough that Hannah had been suckered into working side by side with Isaac at the bake sale booth all morning, but sitting between him and Sammy on the cold concrete curb to watch the parade go by was pure torture. And not just because the high school's horn section sounded like they all had numb lips.

Big Dot was curled up in Isaac's lap and, while she should be glad that her dog wasn't howling along with the unfortunate rendition of "Santa Claus Is Coming to Town" like Kane Chatterson's basset hound, the entire scene was just a bit too cozy for Hannah's taste. A bit too familiar.

The holidays were a time to be with family and loved ones. When she'd been in Ghana, jumping through legal hoops and signing those adoption papers, all she could think of were the happy memories she was going to create for Sammy. All the shared experiences she remembered from her own childhood. Summers on Lake Rush, traditional turkey dinners at the Gregson family's table, Christmas with her dad dressing up as Santa and her mom playing the piano and teaching the kids old-fashioned carols. And how she'd bring some of his country's traditions to celebrate with the rest of their family.

From the time their plane had landed in the States, things hadn't quite worked out according to plan. They'd arrived too late to spend any time on the lake this year. Sammy's first Thanksgiving had been at a hotel buffet in Twin Falls since they'd had to check in early for Luke and Carmen's wedding. And Christmas? Well, Hannah wasn't sure what that'd look like this year with her mom's health. But it was safe to say that she'd never envisioned sitting outside in the freezing cold, next to her ex-boyfriend who was currently teaching her son the tune to "All I Want for Christmas Is My Two Front Teeth."

"Are you going to come to my holiday pageant at school?" Sammy asked Isaac, and Hannah felt her throat close so she was unable to vocalize an objection quickly enough. "It's next week. Mrs. Kamil said I could wear my kente shirt since we're supposed to look fancy when we sing on the stage."

She shot Isaac a panic-stricken look and prayed that he would be too busy to accept the invitation.

Instead, he had the audacity to wiggle his eyebrows at her before replying, "We'll see."

Maybe if Hannah'd acted eager for him to be there, Isaac would've done the opposite and declined. After all, he had a reputation for moving on after he got what he wanted, like the typical spoiled kid who only longed for what he couldn't have.

His past behavior currently had her scratching her head about why he was so eager to be around her today. She'd slept with him last weekend, so why wasn't he moving on now? And why was she allowing herself to dwell on what Isaac was thinking when she should be enjoying the festivities with her son? Probably because her son seemed so determined to include the guy in everything they did.

Fortunately, the clouds soon parted and the sun was blazing down by the time the parade ended, making the weather much more tolerable. Since Monica had come to relieve them at the booth and take over for the afternoon shift, Hannah was able to get some circulation back into her legs by standing up and walking around the outdoor vendor booths in Town Square Park.

Sammy walked right behind her, holding on to Big Dot's leash, which didn't stop the pup from diving between Hannah's feet every few yards. After a few pointed suggestions that Isaac probably had things to do and shouldn't feel obligated to walk with them, the frustrating man increased his efforts at friendliness by offering to hold on to the puppy so Sammy could run ahead and join some of his Cub Scout friends by the thirty-foot-tall spruce on one edge of the park. There was going to be a tree lighting ceremony tonight, and kids were making handcrafted ornaments to hang on the long pine branches.

"Are you guys staying for the concert?" Isaac gestured toward the band setting up on the opposite end of the park, near the gazebo.

"I wasn't planning on it. I have a ton of papers to grade before winter break and Choogie Nguyen invited Sammy for a sleepover." She saw the interest spark in Isaac's eyes and she didn't want him to get the idea that she was going to be all alone this evening. Not that Hannah would mind a repeat performance of what they'd done in that hotel bed, but she wasn't willing to risk all the messy emotions and conversations that would take place afterward. She'd been lucky she'd dodged them for this long. "I mean, I doubt Sammy will make it through the whole night, so I'll probably be picking him up early. But I thought it might be a good idea for him to spend time with another family that's a bit unconventional, like ours."

Isaac nodded. "I think that's a great idea. It's tough being a kid who doesn't necessarily look like everyone else in a new place and wonder where you fit into all of it. It's definitely not the most comforting feeling."

Hannah paused, then turned to look at Isaac, her hands shoved deep into the pockets of her old wool coat. She'd always been interested in knowing more about his parents, but they'd been going through a very drawn out divorce back then and she'd gotten the impression that he didn't want to discuss any of it. He'd also rarely brought up his biracial heritage, and Hannah had followed his lead because she'd told herself that none of that mattered. But in reality it did.

As an adult, especially one who'd lived in another country, she was now more aware of being the only person in a crowd who looked different from everyone else. But she'd been too caught up in her own feelings about her history with Isaac to appreciate that he could be an additional positive influence on her son. "What was it like for you when you came to Sugar Falls that first summer?"

He looped Big Dot's leash in his hand, shortening her lead, and clicked his tongue at the dog before resuming their walk. "It was definitely different than New York City or the boarding school I went to. But I had a double whammy going for me because not only did I look different than many of the kids, but I also came from a different financial background and lived on the East Coast, which made me even more of an outsider. Luckily, I had Uncle Jonesy, who was already well-known and respected here. Kind of like Sammy has you. Luckily, even back then, Sugar Falls tended to be more progressive than other towns I'd visited, so that was a point in my favor."

"You also had your own speedboat. I remember that being a point in your favor, as well."

Isaac's fingers squeezed hers, and she wondered when they'd joined hands. Or if anyone else in the crowd of people walking around them had noticed. "I sure thought it was. But all of that kind of bit me in the butt when I decided to move here for good."

"All of what?"

"My family's money. My reputation. Everyone always assumes that the world has been handed to me on a silver platter. What they didn't know was that my mom was constantly drilling in me this need to rise above all of that and succeed on my own merits."

Hannah gulped. She'd been guilty of that exact thing, but she bit back an apology as he continued. "When I came for the fire chief interview, everybody in town remembered the boat and my dad's private jet. Nobody was interested to find out that I'd built houses for the needy, or served soup at homeless shelters or protested for clean water initiatives, along with everything else that would look good on a college application."

"Is that why you did all that volunteer work? For a college application?"

"That was a low blow." He released her hand, and while she should've been relieved that they no longer had that physical connection on display, she hated the fact that she'd been just as guilty when it came to making assumptions about him.

"Sorry. I didn't mean it to sound like that." She reached out to reclaim his hand. At first his fingers were stiff, much like his jaw, but he didn't pull away.

"If you want to know the truth, I actually did it—and still do it—because it makes me feel good to help others. To know that I made a difference." He paused. "This girl I used to know taught me about giving back to the community."

Hannah's breath caught in her throat. There was no doubt that she was the girl he was referring to, but it was still too soon to talk about what else they'd learned from each other back then. Maybe they should stay focused on what happened to them *after* that fateful summer.

"So I'm guessing you kept up with the volunteer work while you were at Yale?" she asked.

"Yes. And afterward, obviously. I was actually planning to join the Peace Corps after graduating, but at the last minute decided to enlist in the Army."

"Wait. Nobody ever told me you were in the military. Although, I pretty much stayed away from any news about you at all. Whatever happened to you always wanting to be a doctor?"

He shrugged and she wondered if he remembered those late-night talks they used to have about their career paths. The ones where he'd give her a ride home and they'd stay in the truck talking for hours. "I don't know. Being a doctor was a way to appease my mom because

I knew that going to med school would buy me time and allow me to help others before she began pushing me to take over one of the biotech or medical supply companies she'd acquired. But when my parents finally split up, I decided that there was no way I would follow in either of their footsteps and drag out the inevitable. The idea of healing people still appealed to me, but I wanted to be a first responder, to get out to the scene instead of waiting for someone to bring the injuries to me."

"You never did like waiting."

He smiled. "I went through the medic program and it was way more rewarding than anything I'd ever done, but it still felt as though a piece of me was missing. All I could think about was how much I'd loved hearing Uncle Jonesy and Scooter talk about the volunteer fire department. I wanted to give that a try—but when the Army spends that much money on your training, they don't like to reclassify you. So after my four years were up, I went into the National Guard and attended the Fire Academy at Goodfellow Air Force Base in Texas. I'm still in the Reserves."

"How do you manage all that? Being the chief and all the volunteering here in town and then the National Guard on top of it all? Don't you have to go away for training all the time?"

"Once a month. In fact, I go next weekend, but don't worry. I'll be back in time to take you to the Snow Ball."

Her knit ski cap must be covering her ears. "To the what?"

"The Snow Ball. Apparently, Sugar Falls has one every December to celebrate the founding fathers' first winter on the mountain."

"I know what it is. What makes you think I want to go with you?"

"Don't you want to go?"

"I...uh...sure. But, like—go *together*?"

"Yes. Together. Like a real date. And this time, we'll finish whatever we start on the dance floor."

Other than the night of the VFW dinner dance, Isaac couldn't remember the last time he'd had a formal date. When he'd first moved here, he'd gone out a few times with an ER nurse he'd met in Boise, but their conflicting work schedules caused things to quickly fizzle out. Since then, there'd been a few tourists who'd made it clear they were only looking for a vacation fling, yet something just hadn't felt right about taking another woman around the town that held so many memories of Hannah.

Since he was off duty the night of the Snow Ball, he'd foregone the city truck and was navigating his own SUV—his father had had the luxury edition model delivered to fire station the day Isaac became chief, so that everyone in town would remember that Henry Jones's son didn't *need* the job—down the dirt driveway toward her family's cabin. Pulling into the driveway, he tried not to look past the log structure toward the boatshed by the river. Steeling himself to avoid any topics that had to do with their past, he got out of his car and strode to the front door, determined to focus on their future.

Sammy flung the door open before Isaac could knock. Big Dot darted past the boy and was halfway down the front porch steps when Isaac caught the escape artist. Easily scooping the wiggling puppy into one arm, he put the other around Sammy and asked, "Hey, big guy, is your mom here?"

"Yep. So is Chloe," Sammy said. Behind him, Isaac saw one of the teenaged Patrelli girls sitting on the living room sofa, not bothering to look up from her cell phone as her fingers flew over the screen. "She's gonna babysit me so you and Mama can go on your date."

As much as Isaac was pleased by the classification, he was surprised that Hannah had admitted as much to her son. When she'd responded to his text last week about what time he should pick her up, she'd clearly stated that she didn't want Sammy knowing that there was anything going on between them. "Did your mom say we were going on a date?"

"No. But Aunt Kylie and Aunt Carmen both called it that when they were here to help Mama pick out a fancy dress to wear."

"It's more like a playdate," Hannah said as she came down the hallway and entered the living room. "Like the kind Mrs. Meadows is trying to set up with you and Sierra after school next week. Chief Jones and I are just friends."

"Well, Sierra always tries to chase me on the playground at school. She said that if she catches me, she's gonna kiss me. But I'm too fast." Sammy covered his mouth and did a stage whisper to Isaac. "If you chase Mama on your playdate, Chief Isaac, you could probably catch her."

At this, Chloe finally looked up from her phone long enough to glance at Hannah. Then she went right back to typing, speaking as she tapped. "That sure is a fly outfit for just going on a playdate, Miz G."

Isaac's gaze traveled down the length of Hannah's formfitting red dress. Despite the fact that it had long sleeves and hit below her knee, the fabric clung to her every curve and his fingers itched as he thought about peeling it off her.

Hannah pulled on her coat, interrupting his fantasy as she gave the babysitter some last-minute instructions about only using the microwave and where the first-aid kit was. Ten minutes later, Isaac was leaning against the doorframe, jiggling his keys in his pocket as she told Chloe for the eighth time that she would have her cell phone on her and to call if she needed anything.

"I have six younger siblings, Miz G, remember? Me and Sammy will be just fine."

"Sammy and I," the teacher murmured under her breath. "Okay, sweetie, give me a kiss goodbye."

When Isaac finally got Hannah out the door and into his SUV, he climbed behind the wheel and allowed his eyes to roam over the bulky wool coat as he thought of the red knit dress underneath.

It was certainly going to be a long night if she wanted to keep up the "just friends" routine and pretend that this was some sort of playdate. Isaac started the car and stuck to the most neutral of topics as they made small talk on the ten minute drive to the Snow Creek Lodge. Despite the fact that this was their first opportunity to privately discuss their feelings for each other, they shied clear of the subject he knew was on both their minds. He asked her about the kids in her class, she asked him about his Reserves training weekend. They talked about themselves without really talking about themselves.

And Isaac wasn't about to push for more. Mostly because he wasn't sure what else he wanted from her. Or, more importantly, what she wanted from *him*.

"This feels weird," Hannah finally said as they sat in his vehicle in the parking lot, watching the other couples walk toward the entrance.

"What does?" he asked, already knowing exactly what she'd meant.

Hannah shifted in the leather passenger seat to face

him. "I don't remember us ever really going on a planned date. At least, not to anywhere formal."

They'd been friends first, despite the fact that Isaac had always wanted to be more. Just when things finally started getting serious, they'd both had to go home for their senior year. The summer after graduation, it had been like they were getting to know each other all over again. Then, as quickly as their relationship had turned physical, it turned into nothing at all.

"I had a similar thought when I pulled up to your house," Isaac admitted. "But then you told Sammy it wasn't a real date."

She leaned back against the headrest. "That's because I don't know what it is."

"What do you want it to be?"

"I just don't want it to be awkward anymore. Or for people to keep bringing up what happened between us all those years ago."

"Hell, Hannah, even *we* don't talk about what happened between us all those years ago."

"Then let's make a deal tonight. No more awkwardness. We put away all that stuff from our past and refuse to give anyone in this town a reason to bring it up."

"Deal." He stuck out his palm to cement their truce with a handshake. He would've pulled her toward him to seal it with a kiss, but a knock on the passenger window caused them to jump apart.

"Hey, you two." Scooter Deets knocked a second time, then cupped his gnarled hands around his eyes and peered inside. "Let's get inside and boogie!"

Hannah was relieved that Isaac wasn't the boogieing type, since being on the dance floor would've put them at the center of attention. Although after a couple of hours and two Mistletoe Martinis, even she was swaying along to the music. Big Rhonda and the Roadsters had a long and diverse repertoire and were a Sugar Falls staple, playing at every local event. They'd not only performed that night at the VFW, but they'd also doubled as the Dixieland Quintet for the Ski Potato Festival. Tonight, though, the members had swapped out their punk-rock attire and seersucker suits for matching elf costumes.

Cessy Walker and her Snow Ball committee had gone all out with the white and silver decorations, turning the grand ballroom of the ritzy Snow Creek Lodge into a sparkling ice palace, minus the ice. In fact, with all the merriment and dancing and pressed-in bodies of at least four hundred townspeople, it was downright warm in there.

Hannah tugged on the neck of the red knit dress she'd borrowed from her sister-in-law. Just like before, she'd been misled by the long sleeves and below-the-knee hem, thinking that this had been the more modest option in Kylie's closet. What Hannah hadn't taken into account was that the dress would fit her like a glove, and despite the fact that she wasn't showing any skin, the cut didn't leave much to the imagination. It was also made of some sort of wool and cashmere blend, which, coupled with the cranberry and vodka cocktail warming her blood, had Hannah suddenly feeling the need to cool down.

Of course, it also didn't help that Isaac had his arm casually draped over the back of Hannah's chair, his long, deft fingers hidden under the loose waves of her hair as he stroked the nape of her neck and spoke to several other firefighters and paramedics seated at their table.

A couple of hours ago, when she'd suggested that they put aside their past and all the awkward baggage that came along with it, she hadn't meant they should go in the complete opposite direction, either—putting their current feelings out there for everyone to comment upon. Despite the curious looks and whispered comments that were still floating their way, her head was at risk of falling back dreamily as his magical fingers drove her to distraction. It would be so easy to just say *to hell with it* and fall completely into his arms.

But she had her son to think of. Sammy was still adapting to living in a new place, surrounded by new people and a completely different culture. He didn't need the added stress of hearing the playground rumors—since gossip happened at all ages—about his mother and her questionable behavior with her old fling. No matter how carefully she'd tried to shield Sammy from the stressors going on her life, kids were intuitive and could pick up on things like that. Just look at the way he'd been reluctant to bond with her mother, how he sensed her fragility and was clearly frightened by it. It was important that Sammy think everything was hunky-dory when Hannah's whole world had gone completely topsy-turvy.

Yes, the heat of the room was getting to her, and it wasn't helping that the constant barrage of thoughts racing through her mind kept going back to whether or not being here with Isaac was a mistake. Whether dating Isaac Jones would be too much to take on.

"I think I'm going to step out onto the terrace and get some fresh air," she whispered into Isaac's ear.

"I'll come with you," he offered, but she put a reassuring palm on his arm as she scooted her chair back. Even under his crisp, striped dress shirt, she could feel the outline of his rounded biceps.

"No, stay and visit with your friends. I'll be right back."

Hannah wove through the crowd, making her way to

the French doors that led out to the cobblestone terrace. Several other partygoers must've had the same idea and were standing near the massive stone firepit in the center. But Hannah wasn't up to making any more small talk. In fact, she set out toward the low-walled perimeter where the lack of twinkling lights provided more shadows and less chance of running into someone else. As she navigated the uneven ground in her borrowed black suede heels, she began thinking that maybe she should take a break from volunteering and socializing and everything else she'd been cramming onto her already full plate. There were plenty of other endeavors Hannah could be dedicating her time to. Like seeing her mother more often. The doctors said it could be five months or five years. Nobody knew how long she had left.

Hannah was brainstorming ways to get Sammy and her mom together when another voice from her past stopped her in her tracks. "Long time no see, Gregson."

Carter Mahoney.

Chapter Fifteen

Her heart lightened as she pivoted, a welcoming smile on her face.

"Hey, Carter. How've you been?" Hannah asked, stepping into his arms for a hug hello, just as she'd done many times that first semester they'd been at college together.

"Busy." He squeezed her in response, but instead of the brief contact putting her at ease, she could feel the hair on her arms lifting to attention underneath her long sleeves. She withdrew from the embrace first, feeling someone's eyes on her back as Carter continued speaking, unfazed. "I haven't had a vacation in almost three years, but my dad is slowing down so I took a couple weeks off to fly home and spend time with him for the holidays. Glad to see some things around here haven't changed."

"Actually…" Isaac's deep voice intruded on them in the dark. "Some things around here have changed quite a bit."

"Isaac Jones." Carter's voice sounded pleasant enough, but her old friend's raised brows were directed at Hannah, silently asking plenty of questions. Instead of accepting Carter's outstretched hand, Isaac put his arm around Hannah's shoulders, drawing her to his side.

Neither she nor Isaac were wearing their coats and it was easy to feel the tautness of his tense muscles, the flexing of his biceps behind her shoulder. Now she knew why she'd had that apprehensive feeling when she'd first seen Carter. He and Isaac had never seemed to like each other, a quiet sense of competition always lingering under the surface any time they were in the same place. However, all of that shouldn't matter now that they were grown men, both successful in their own lives. Or, at least, Hannah assumed Carter was doing well, based on the small glimpses of him she'd seen over the years on social media. They'd lost contact after he transferred to a different college.

Isaac leaned in even closer as his eyes narrowed in Carter's direction, as though he was sizing up an opponent. When he was apparently done, he turned to Hannah and brushed one of her loose curls behind her ear before saying, "Why don't we go dance?"

Okay, now she knew that something was definitely up. Not only did he hate dancing, she was pretty sure that he was throwing menacing looks over his shoulder at Carter as she allowed Isaac to guide her back toward the ballroom.

"What was that all about?" she finally asked when he pulled her into his arms on the dance floor and they were close enough that nobody would be able to overhear them.

"I never did like that guy," Isaac replied, his hands settling on her lower back.

"Yeah, I picked up on that vibe. But why were you so

rude? You didn't even shake his hand before dragging me inside. If I didn't know better, I'd think you were getting territorial…"

His eyes finally stopped appraising the other couples around them and zeroed in on her. But he didn't deny anything.

"That's it, isn't it?" she asked, her palms pressing against Isaac's chest so that she could lean back and read his face. "You're trying to lay some sort of claim to me. In front of Carter Mahoney, of all people."

"I don't think anyone here could blame me for that," he said, and Hannah realized that they were no longer swaying to the music or even making a pretense at dancing.

Nor were Elaine Marconi or Marcia Duncan or several other people standing along the edge of the dance floor. In fact, it was as if a crowd was forming around her and Isaac, making Hannah's flight instinct rage inside her.

He'd made a deal to try and act normal. To not draw any more attention to them. Yet they were standing in the center of a circle of people, people who were watching them and murmuring out of the sides of their mouths, most likely eager to witness some sort of show. Why did the ballroom of the Snow Creek Lodge suddenly feel like the center ring for a heavyweight title match?

"Maybe we should talk about this somewhere else," she said between clenched teeth, despite the fact that she would've preferred not to talk about it at all. He was stiff and his jaw was set as he looked past her toward the terrace doors. Something was clearly wrong with Isaac and everyone else in town seemed to be clued in to what it might be, but Hannah was at a complete loss and she hated being at a disadvantage. Her skin was on fire, and not in a good way. She spotted the clock near the coat check area and latched onto the one thing in her world that made sense. "I've got to get home to Sammy."

"But we're just getting to the good part, now that Carter's here," Elaine Marconi said before letting out a tittering hiccup. Hannah attempted a scathing look in her direction, but the woman only smirked before throwing back the rest of the wine in her glass.

Isaac lifted his hand from Hannah's waist and glanced at his wristwatch. He probably was well aware of the fact that the babysitter wasn't expecting her home for another hour, but he didn't protest. Somebody behind them let out a giggle, but it didn't affect her nearly as much as the weight of Isaac's gaze as he studied her. His voice was low and cautious when he said, "People are going to talk about us if we leave now."

It seemed to Hannah that people were going to talk regardless. The best thing she could do was get out of here before making whatever this was into a bigger show. Before she was forced to relive those humiliating months when she'd been the sole subject of the town's titillating entertainment. Isaac had flown home that Labor Day weekend—or so she'd heard—leaving Hannah to deal with the aftermath of their breakup all alone.

She never used to worry about what others thought of her, but then Isaac Jones came along. Her skin prickled with anger at him for making her feel this way and anger at herself for succumbing to it.

"Then you can stay," she offered as she inched back, trying to draw as little attention to herself as she could. "I'll catch a cab."

He arched a dark eyebrow. "A cab? In Sugar Falls?"

He had her there. The town wasn't exactly big enough to necessitate a cab company, let alone a single cab. She doubted Uber had made it to Sugar Falls since she'd been gone. Lifting her chin, she said, "Don't worry about me. I can always find a ride with someone."

If she hadn't been looking right into Isaac's face, she would've missed the slight flaring of his nostrils. She turned toward the door, not wanting to care about why her words had bothered him. The band had just finished the last bars of the slow song and Hannah was only ten feet away when he called out, "Maybe you can ask Carter Mahoney? I seem to recall him always being available to give you a ride."

Hannah's entire body recoiled at the implication as several gasps sounded across the dance floor. Sure, she'd always been a fighter, but it was different when the cause wasn't her own. Five minutes ago, Hannah would've been rooted to the spot, waiting for a sinkhole to open up and swallow her right then and there. Now, she was past the point of caring about a scene. Hannah had a son and a career and a reputation to fight for. And she also had the sudden image of Elaine's smug face swimming in front of her.

"Here we go," Elaine said to nobody in particular, but the woman's eyes were bulging out of her head with excitement at the merest hint of scandal.

Hannah's shoulders went back and her spine went ramrod straight as she turned back to Isaac. "What's that supposed to mean?"

"It means that you always seem to run to him whenever you're done with me."

"Done with *you*?" Hannah closed the distance between them, feeling like a wild animal stalking her prey. She wasn't quite sure what Carter had to do with anything, but there was no mistaking that Isaac was bringing up the past. Too bad he was clearly misremembering how things had gone down between them. Luckily, she was ready to set him straight. "If I recall, *you're* the one who moved on and bragged about it. You got what you wanted back then and you got what you wanted the night of my brother's wed—"

"Okay, tiger." Drew appeared at her side and wrapped a steely arm around Hannah's waist. Drew was the calm brother, the voice of reason. He would never have bid on her ex-boyfriend at a bachelor auction and then invited the guy to his wedding. He also, apparently, wouldn't stand by and let his little sister make a fool of herself. "Let's let it go for tonight."

She resisted at first, determined to finish what she'd been about to say. But the intense look on Drew's serious face warned against it. Instead, Hannah let her brother lead her toward the exit, thankful that his long strides helped to hide the wobble in her legs.

When they got to Drew's car in the parking lot, Hannah rounded on him. "I've been waiting ten years to tell Isaac Jones off and you yanked me out of there right when I get to the good part."

"Isaac's an idiot," Drew mumbled under his breath. The statement caught Hannah off guard, only because she was spoiling for an argument.

She tilted her head. "Well, there's no disputing that point."

"Oh, you're an idiot, too," Drew said, and Hannah's eyes rounded as her mouth sputtered.

"Is that your clinical assessment, Dr. Gregson?" Hannah put her hands on her hips, all her anger redirected at her psychologist brother.

"Yes, it is. And since you value my professional advice, I'm going to tell you the same thing everyone else has been telling you both. You and Isaac need to make peace with the past. And by making peace, I don't mean telling him off in front of the whole town. If you can't avoid making a scene, then maybe you should try and stay away from each other."

"Make peace? You may not remember this, since you were away at college, but I made peace with him in my own way." By refusing to let anyone bring up the name Isaac Jones in her presence.

"I hate to point out the obvious, but you two weren't exactly being peaceful back there on the dance floor."

"Maybe because *he* hasn't made peace with it." Hannah pointed toward the entrance of the Snow Creek Lodge. "You heard him bring up Carter, right?"

"I did. As did the rest of the town. But airing your dirty laundry for the entire world to see is what got you two into this situation in the first place."

Hannah felt her lips turn down in a pout. She hated when one of her brothers was right.

Isaac pulled out of the Snow Creek Lodge parking lot and flew down the highway. Seeing Carter Mahoney tonight had brought back too many unresolved memories, but seeing Hannah standing in the arms of Isaac's former adversary was more than he'd been able to take.

He'd made an ass of himself, the way he'd refused to shake Carter's hand then laid claim to Hannah, wrapping a possessive arm around her before steering her to the dance floor. Isaac hated how weak it made him seem, to be so bothered by another man's mere presence around her. But it had also been his own insecurities driving him. His own need to be her number one guy. Hannah had immediately picked up on his discomfort, but then she'd acted as though she couldn't imagine why he would possibly have a problem with Carter.

As he drove toward her house, he cursed himself for

making that comment about Carter always giving her a ride. It had been a cheap shot and he wasn't proud of it, but coming face-to-face with the man she'd once left him for had a tendency to bring out the worst in Isaac.

The needle of his speedometer continued to rise, along with all the old anger and hurt he'd thought he'd let go of long ago. When would Hannah figure out that Isaac had been the best man for her? Or at least better than that damn Carter Mahoney.

Isaac recognized the SUV pulling out of her long driveway. His pulse slowed briefly as he braked to prepare for the turn. At least it had been Drew who'd driven Hannah home and not Carter. After her brother yanked Hannah away before either of them could cause more of a scene, Isaac had started after her but been waylaid by Jonesy who'd cautioned him that it would be best to let everyone simmer down. He'd taken his uncle's advice—for a full thirty minutes—before climbing into his SUV and heading this way.

The beam of his headlights bounced off the front of Hannah's cabin as his vehicle bumped along the dirt driveway. There was a fresh dusting of snow on the porch steps and it surprised Isaac to realize that it had been falling the entire drive here. He was a first responder. The one who got called out to the scene of a crash after a distracted driver took a turn too sharply. Yet he'd been on the road for ten miles and hadn't even noticed the weather conditions.

Instead of scolding himself about the dangers of tunnel vision, he soldiered on, getting out and walking to her front door, convinced that his dangerous oversight was all the more reason to finally get this much needed conversation out of his system once and for all. Although she must've had the same idea, because she chose that exact second to step out onto her front porch.

He paused, his dress shoes crunching on the fresh snow beneath his feet. If she was beautiful when she was happy and carefree and helping others, then Hannah Gregson was downright stunning when she was angry.

Watching her, reckless determination faded away, leaving nothing but confusion and an attraction that was too strong to resist. Did he really want to do this? Should he confront her and force them both to relive every way they'd caused each other pain? Or should he just let old hurts die?

"What are you doing here?" she asked. The wintery air and the shape of her snug red dress made her breasts all the more prominent, her erect nipples drawing his attention away from the angry line of her normally full lips. Before he could get his tongue untwisted, she added, "Sammy is sleeping on the sofa."

Her words—along with her position blocking the front door, both hands on her hips—were a warning that she wasn't about to let him inside her house, no matter how frozen she must be, facing off against him without a coat. That was fine with him. If she wanted to square off and do battle with him out here, then he'd say his piece and leave.

"I think we both know why I'm here, Hannah. No more pretending that everything is okay between us. If we're going to have to live in the same town, then let's get it all out in the open now."

She took a deep breath; a cloud of condensation puffed out of her mouth as she released it. But she didn't say anything, as though the first person to show their cards would no longer have the upper hand.

"Fine, I'll start," he said, stepping up onto the porch

so they'd be on equal ground. "You've always acted like you were better than everyone else."

"Me?" Hannah lifted her hands to either side of her temples. "What about you? Ever since you were sixteen, you've been a constant show-off. Always trying to prove to everyone how wonderful you are."

"Well, most people can see that I am a pretty decent guy once they finally give me a chance. But for some reason, you've always been too damn stubborn to see it."

"Oh, I saw you getting plenty of chances ten years ago when Elaine made it a point to mention how many girls you'd taken out on that stupid speedboat the day after I gave you my virginity."

"Elaine? You mean the same person who told *me* that you were bragging to everyone who would listen that you could do much better than some spoiled rich boy who thought the world revolved around him? You even proved it by letting Carter Mahoney drive you home that same night."

Hannah's eyebrows slammed together. "Carter was trying to console me."

"Yeah, he had quite the reputation for consoling girls belowdecks on his daddy's fishing boat."

"If I recall, your reputation with females wasn't much better."

That stung. "I never asked for that reputation."

"Are you saying that it wasn't well earned?"

Isaac jerked his thumb toward the old wooden structure near the edge of the river. "Hannah, you weren't the only virgin the night we slept together in that boatshed."

Chapter Sixteen

Hannah's mouth opened and closed twice as she studied him. "You never told me."

"Hi, Chief Isaac," Sammy said, and Hannah pivoted in surprise as though they'd just been caught red-handed in the midst of a make-out session. "Did you and Mama have fun on your date?"

"Hi, big guy," Isaac said to her son, always seeming so casual and relaxed around the boy when Hannah was raging inside.

"It wasn't a…" Hannah sighed, unable to finish saying it had only been a playdate. It was as though the appearance of her son had suddenly taken some of the wind out of her sails. Or maybe it was Isaac's admission that he hadn't been quite the playboy she'd once believed. Either way, all the heat and anger had left Hannah's body and she shivered, wrapping one arm around her middle.

"Sweetie, it's too cold to be outside here in just your pajamas."

"But you don't have your jacket, either. Did you leave it on your date?"

Hannah didn't know where she'd left it. Probably the same place she'd left her pride. "I must have. Go inside, Sammy, and I'll be there in just a second."

Her son padded back into the house in his bare feet and Hannah felt guilt wash through her. She didn't want the boy to think he was in trouble or had done anything wrong. But she could only deal with one offended male at a time.

"I didn't know that you hadn't been with anyone else, Isaac," she said in a hushed voice by way of apology. "You were supposed to pick me up for the bonfire the next day and you never showed up. When I finally got a lift out to Honey Point, I saw you racing by with your wakeboard tow bar and four pretty girls. Less than twenty-four hours after you'd slept with me."

The echo of their past ricocheted between them on that front porch, and now that the accusations were finally out there, Hannah couldn't take them back.

"I'd been out fishing—alone—that afternoon, and a stupid tourist on a Jet Ski ran into the back of my boat while I was anchored. He dented my propeller and I was stuck waiting for someone from the marina to bring me a spare one. It was the wrong size and I had to sit there another hour to get the right one. My cell battery died while I was waiting, then it took forever for me to change the propeller out. On my way back to the dock, I saw Marcia and a few of her friends who'd run out of gas. I was going to tow them in, but she was afraid her dad would find out that she'd forgotten to fuel up so I gave them a ride to the pumps. I used one of their phones to call you, but you never answered."

"Well, what was I supposed to think? When you drove by, all of them were waving and blasting music, and it seemed like quite the party. Elaine was standing next to me and asked if I'd already added my bikini top to your collection. She made it sound like I was just another one of your conquests."

"And you listened to *Elaine*?"

She sighed. "Maybe I shouldn't have, but that little video you made later that night pretty much confirmed that things were over between us."

"First of all, I never made that video."

"Really, Isaac? Because it looked and sounded exactly like you."

"I mean, obviously, it was me in it, but I didn't know that Elaine was recording me. And I sure as hell didn't post it."

"But the fact remains that I trusted you with my heart and you told anyone who would listen that I was using you before moving on to the next guy."

"What was I supposed to think? I finally got to Honey Point just in time to see you sailing off into the sunset with Carter Mahoney."

"I was upset, Isaac. Carter was only giving me a ride home. We've never been anything but friends."

"Well, I was upset, too." Isaac crossed his arms in front of his chest.

"You had nothing to be upset about."

"Elaine told me that you called me a spoiled rich kid who wasn't worth your time before you took off with Carter."

Hannah's cheeks flamed at the quote. "I might've said something like that when I saw you with all the girls."

"And you left it up to Elaine to tell me that it was over?"

"No, Isaac. I would've told you myself. That part about it being over, she must've added on her own."

"Well, from where I was standing, it looked like she was right. That you were moving on to the next guy."

"I was never moving on to the next guy." Hannah let out a frustrated huff. After ten years, she had still never allowed a guy to take Isaac's place in her heart. "I was only thinking of getting away from the bonfire. Of getting away from all the gossip. There was never anything going on between me and Carter. He only offered me an escape."

Isaac winced and she could tell by the hurt reflected in his eyes that her words had landed an unintended blow. "An escape from me? Was that what you wanted?"

"Of course not. I wanted *you*."

"Then why didn't you fight for me?"

She sucked in her cheeks, a lump rising in her throat. He was right. She could stand up and fight like hell when it came to everyone's needs but her own. She lifted her shoulders, then dropped them. "I didn't see you fighting for me, either, Isaac."

"Maybe I should've followed you that night and confronted you myself about the breakup, rather than drinking straight from the bottle of Captain Morgan someone was passing around. But I was a prideful, stupid kid back then and didn't want to believe that I'd come in second place. By the time I came to my senses the next morning and finally stopped puking, I did drive over here with a raging headache and a wilted bouquet of peonies to win you back. When I got here, though, Carter's truck was in the driveway. What was I supposed to think?"

A wave of nausea roiled through her. She'd had no idea

that Isaac had tried to make amends back then. Just like him, she'd been willing to assume the worst. Her voice was low and filled with resignation as she tried to explain. "Carter came that morning to show me the video. To warn me that everyone was talking about us."

"Listen, I hated myself for that video. Not just because it made me look like a fool, but because I knew it would hurt you. I had no idea I was being recorded or I never would've opened my mouth. Those things I said? I didn't mean them. A million times I've wished I could take them back. I loved you, but instead of proving it, I lashed out in anger and hurt."

Loved. Past tense. That extra D hung in the frosty, December air between them.

Hannah's sigh let out a cloud of her warm breath, like pressurized steam leaving her body, until she felt empty and drained. "We were just kids back then. We didn't know what love was."

"Do we know what it is now?" Isaac asked.

"I know what it *isn't*. It isn't jealousy and bitterness and jumping to conclusions."

"You're absolutely right," he said and she saw the drop in his shoulders, the tension draining from the lines around his mouth as though he was giving up. He glanced back at his SUV, still idling in her driveway, ready for him to turn away from her and drive straight out of her life. It caught Hannah off guard when, instead of beating a hasty retreat, Isaac asked, "Have you been in love since then?"

Hannah looked down at the black suede pumps that would've been pinching her toes if her feet weren't completely numb from the cold. When she lifted her eyes, she gave a slight shake of her head. "Have you?"

But before he could answer, Sammy cracked the door

open again and tugged at her hand. "Mama, I can't fall asleep."

It was a reminder of all the other pressing responsibilities Hannah had waiting for her. Her son. Her mother. She looked at Isaac, her eyes pleading with him to just let everything go. To let her go. "I can't do this anymore."

His jaw was firm, his stubborn chin set, his brown eyes dejected when he gave a barely perceptible nod. Isaac reached passed her and squeezed Sammy's shoulder. "See you around town, big guy."

And, just like that, Isaac Jones turned around and walked out of her life again.

He heard the dog's bark before Clausson knocked on Isaac's open office door on Wednesday afternoon. "You have visitors, Chief."

It had only been a week since he'd driven away from Hannah's cabin after she shut him out for the second and final time. She'd made it clear that they were through, that she couldn't keep seeing him. And really, it was for the best. His heart had already been through one major breakup with her and he still hadn't gotten over it.

But that didn't stop his pulse from springing to life with fresh hope when he heard Sammy's voice speaking to Garcia in the TV lounge. Isaac paused outside the room, steeling his thoughts from getting too full of promises for what could never be. Or could it?

He turned the corner, fully expecting to see Hannah, then stopped in his tracks when his eyes landed on Donna Gregson, instead. Her thin frame was bundled up in a puffy purple coat over a sweat suit that could've easily been mistaken for a pair of pajamas. On her head, she wore a pink ball cap that said Fight Like a Girl. His medic training had him giving the woman a once-over for any signs of discomfort or impairment. She looked healthy, despite the fact that she was battling a terminal illness, and he had to wonder what would bring her into the fire station on one of the coldest days in December.

Then he saw Sammy and Big Dot and knew. The woman was here to appease her grandson. The same grandson who was too afraid to get close to her for fear that she was dying.

"Hey, Chief Isaac," Sammy said, dropping the leash to give him a wave. "Grammie said that if Big Dot wants to be a fire dog, she needs to spend more time at the station to get trained."

"I wasn't aware we were training any new fire dogs today." Isaac lifted a questioning brow at Mrs. Gregson. "Or ever."

What Isaac really wanted to ask was, *Does your daughter know about this?* Hannah's mom didn't rise to the bait, though. In fact, she kept her expression completely neutral, a skill she must've developed as a minister's wife who helped counsel her husband's flock. When he was eighteen and would go to their cabin to drop off Hannah, Mrs. Gregson had always had the ability to set Isaac on edge with that same look. Back then he never knew what the woman thought of him. And, apparently, he still didn't.

While it wasn't fair to question Sammy about what his mother knew or the motive for their visit, Isaac still found himself turning to the child, searching for a clue about what they were doing there. Especially since, last he'd heard, Hannah wasn't exactly comfortable leaving Sammy with Mrs. Gregson due to the woman's growing health issues and the fragility of the boy's bond with her.

But instead of providing Isaac with answers, Sammy's lower lip quivered as though he'd done something wrong.

Shame threaded through Isaac for making the boy feel badly.

"Not that we're opposed to having the right candidate." Isaac knelt between him and the rambunctious pup, who was playing a game of tug-of-war with herself. And losing. He scratched between Big Dot's ears and she made growling sounds as she clenched her leash between her tiny teeth. "If she's indeed trainable."

"She is." Sammy eagerly bobbed his head. "Right, Grammie?"

"Everyone is trainable, if given the right incentive," Mrs. Gregson replied, her unreadable gaze never leaving Isaac. "Even old dogs."

"Speaking of old dogs…" Isaac stood up. "Uncle Jonesy might have some leftover bacon in the kitchen that you can use as treats. Clausson, why don't you take Sammy and our new candidate here back to the kitchen to work on some simple commands?"

The dog's ears perked up at the mention of bacon and Sammy barely recaptured the leash before she pulled him along behind her, Clausson following them both.

"Mind if I sit down?" Donna Gregson nodded toward one of the recliners.

"Of course. Sorry, I should've offered you a seat earlier."

"I get enough of everyone else treating me like a frail invalid." She flicked her wrist at him. "I don't need it from you, too."

"Then you won't mind me asking why you're here." Isaac walked over to one of the side tables, picked up the remote control and turned off the fishing channel on the big-screen TV.

"Because Sammy is obsessed with firefighters and fire departments and turning that handful of a puppy into an honorary fire dog—whatever that is." Donna Gregson lifted the lever on the side of her recliner, propping her feet up. Apparently not planning on leaving anytime soon. "And because my daughter is just as stubborn as she is selfless. And she tends to know what's best for everyone but herself."

Isaac dropped into the matching chair next to hers, the woman's surprising comment all but knocking him off his feet. "So, I'm guessing Hannah doesn't know you're here."

"Are you kidding? She would be mortified if she found out. Not that Sammy won't tell her as soon as she gets home."

Good. At least he wouldn't have to worry about keeping this little meeting a secret. Isaac had a lot of questions on the tip of his tongue, but the one that made it out first was, "Where is she?"

"Shopping for Christmas presents in Boise. School's out for the winter break and she dropped Sammy and Big Dot off at our house down there so she could go buy his gifts."

"Should you be driving up the mountain in your condition?"

She narrowed her eyes and Isaac wished he hadn't brought up her health again. "You guys have ambulances and medically trained staff here, don't you?"

He nodded.

"Then I should be in good hands. Besides. I'm actually having a pretty good day. I wouldn't drive over here with Sammy if I wasn't feeling up to it. Now, do you want to talk about my cancer or do you want to talk about my daughter?"

That was a loaded question if Isaac had ever heard one. He didn't want to be an insensitive jerk who was willing to ignore the poor woman's medical needs, but his curiosity was killing him. The past week, he'd been walking around town with his ears wide open, hoping for even the slightest bit of information about Hannah and how she was doing. Yet any time he walked into a store or restaurant, all the chattering ceased and everyone watched him with keen interest, probably wanting to be the first to pick up on any new developments in his destroyed relationship.

"I want to talk about whatever brought you here," he offered.

"Good. My daughter has been in a funk ever since you showed up back in Sugar Falls."

"Just to be clear, ma'am, I was here first. She came home after I arrived."

"Son, I don't know how many more months I have left on this earth, and you want to argue semantics?"

Isaac sank lower in his recliner, a petulant child being called to task. "So Hannah's been annoyed since we ran into each again. Are you here to ask me to leave town?"

"My husband and my sons told me I'd have my work cut out with you both." Mrs. Gregson shook her head, then straightened the brim of her cap before she continued. "For two people with such charitable hearts, you each have a reckless amount of pride when it comes to believing in each other."

"Who says that I don't believe your daughter? In fact, just the other night, she told me that she couldn't see me anymore. I believed her and I'm trying to do my best to let her go."

"That's the problem. You're both trying to let go when you should be holding on tight."

"Holding on tight to a relationship that she doesn't want?"

"It's not the relationship she doesn't want. It's the hurt." Donna Gregson held up her hand when Isaac opened his mouth to apologize for all the emotional destruction he'd caused way back then. "I know you were nothing but a kid yourself when that stupid video came out, and from what I've been able to pick up from my sources, you've done your best to make amends for all of that."

It was true. Over the years, long after they'd gone their separate ways, he'd thought about that video from time to time with a twinge of remorse, making him double down on his public service and volunteerism as a way to prove to others—and to himself—that he maybe he wasn't a bad person, after all.

"Who are your sources?" he asked. And where had they been when he needed them to tell Hannah all of this?

"Sugar Falls is a small town. Even for us summer folks. Everyone talked about your breakup back then and everyone is talking today about whether you two will end up back together."

"It was always the rumors that got us, you know?" He let his head fall against the leather headrest, sending a pent-up breath toward the ceiling. "I think she's worried about her reputation and how it might affect Sammy and her job at the school. What she doesn't realize is that most of the people in this town, including me, think she walks on water."

"My daughter is a saint," Mrs. Gregson agreed. "Always taking care of people and volunteering for everything under the sun. But she can be pigheaded and downright blind when it comes to looking out for herself. Not that I blame her hesitation where you're concerned.

I get it that she doesn't want to get hurt again. Or made to look like a fool."

"I think we can safely say that neither one of us wants that." Back then, Isaac had been the injured party. Or, at least, he'd thought so. When he'd heard from his Uncle Jonesy that Carter brought Hannah home for Thanksgiving their freshman year of college, he had never been more convinced that she'd intended to leave Isaac all along. But now, faced with his own actions and inactions, his own contributions to the destruction of their relationship, he wasn't sure how to overcome the damage they'd already inflicted. "Are you here to warn me off, then? To tell me to stay away from your daughter?"

Mrs. Gregson brought her palms together, bowed her head and murmured something that sounded like, "Lord, give me patience."

Since she obviously wasn't talking to Isaac, he remained silent and tried to sort out what pieces he was missing from this puzzle. But his reprieve only lasted seconds before she lifted her eyes to him and said, "I think I'm going to need reinforcements to get through to you both."

"What do you mean?"

"I mean that I want to see my daughter happy before I die and I think that being with you will make her happy. She loved you once and I know it's still there, buried beneath all the heartache and disillusionment. But it's going to take more than just a dying wish to get her to see past all that."

It would've been easy to ask Mrs. Gregson why she was assuming that he might still have feelings for Hannah or whether he was even interested in making her daughter happy. But the question would've been pointless because they both knew the truth. Actually, everyone in town probably did.

Instead of protesting, he asked, "What do you suggest?"

When Hannah's dad told her that Sammy and her mother had driven up to Sugar Falls, Hannah hopped back into her car and floored it up the highway. Her mom's phone went straight to voice mail, and when Hannah called the landline at the cabin, there was no answer.

Unfortunately, the check fuel light came on several miles before she reached town and she was forced to stop at the Gas 'N Mart. The credit card machine on the pump was out of order and she growled in frustration. The place was owned by Elaine Marconi and her husband, making Hannah send up a silent prayer that it would be Chuck who was on duty this evening.

She entered the mini-mart with her wallet and decided that fate was not on her side today. Elaine sat beside the register, a tabloid magazine open on the counter. However, the woman's eyes weren't bothering to look at printed gossip when the opportunity for the live stuff had just walked into her store.

"Hey there, Hannah. What's going on?"

"Not much." Hannah didn't even bother to keep the irritation from her voice as she handed over a twenty dollar bill. It was all the cash she had, but she wasn't about to use her credit card inside and have to come back in to get the receipt. "I'm on pump number four."

Elaine's bracelets jingled as she pushed the buttons on the register and Hannah quickly turned toward the exit. "What's the rush? You have a hot date or something?"

Every word she and Isaac had said to each other last week came floating back to Hannah. Every tear she'd cried back then, every assumption she'd made, had originated with this woman. Hannah's shoulders reared back and she turned around to point her anger and frustration in the direction it should've gone ten years ago.

"Why are you such a nosy troublemaker, Elaine?"

Instead of acting offended, Elaine smiled and took a drink out of a paper slushee cup that smelled suspiciously of pinot grigio. "Because life would be boring if people like me didn't spice it up."

Disgust threatened to choke Hannah and she shivered instead. "Do you realize all the lives you've affected with your gossip over the years?"

"Is that what's bothering you?" Elaine asked. "Something I might've said back when we were teenagers? Really, Hannah, you give me too much credit. I only said what everyone was thinking. Including you."

Was that true? Had Hannah really thought those same things about Isaac all those years ago? That he was adding bikini tops to his collection?

It wasn't that she hadn't trusted him, but she *had* been quick to doubt him. Just like he'd been quick to doubt her. How much easier would it have been to ignore everyone else and go to him? To have asked for an explanation and believed him? To have believed each other?

Staring at Elaine's smug expression, something clicked in Hannah's mind. The woman was right. By letting another person's comments affect her, she'd given someone else way too much power in her relationship. Way too much power in her life.

That ended tonight. A weight was lifted from Hannah's shoulders as she decided that she would stop caring about what the gossips said and take her future back.

Chapter Seventeen

Isaac stood outside of Luke Gregson's old Victorian home on Pinecone Avenue, the lights inside not doing much to brighten the darkness in his heart. When he'd asked Donna Gregson for her suggestion on how to win back Hannah, the last thing he'd expected was an invitation to their family dinner on Christmas Eve a couple of days later.

Standing outside on the recently shoveled porch, he waged a war with himself, debating whether or not he should go inside. He shivered underneath his heavy fleece-lined coat, his feet telling him he needed to make a decision soon before he froze to death out here in the frost. How had he made it to age twenty-eight and never once attended a big family holiday gathering like this?

Growing up an only child, his experience with Christmas parties had always been grand, formal affairs with his parents and their wealthy friends. The gifts he usually received had been motivational books from his mom and over-the-top toys from his dad—which was always bittersweet because there'd never been any other kids around with whom to enjoy them. But judging from the shrieks of laughter coming from the other side of the door, there were plenty of children in attendance tonight. Which meant lots of Gregsons. And lots of Gregsons meant lots of judgmental, questioning looks—and protective big brothers.

He took a step back, calculating the distance from the front door to his SUV. But his retreat was blown when a little face pressed up to the frosted glass window pane.

"Chief Isaac is here," a young voice called out, and there were several thuds against the front door before it opened to reveal Sammy and his cousin Aiden.

The boys grabbed each of his hands to tug him across the threshold and he was suddenly thrust into a room of complete chaos. A set of toddler twins in matching red velvet dresses, waddled like ducks amidst the shredded wrapping paper and ribbons littering the floor, along with a slew of opened boxes and toys. There were adults, as well, but Isaac wasn't quite ready to focus on who was where because then he'd find himself seeking out Hannah. And he didn't know if he was ready for that confrontation yet.

Or if she even knew that he was coming.

Instead, he focused on the huge noble fir in the middle of the room, the steepled ceiling providing the only location that would tolerate its ten foot plus height. The tree back at the station was artificial and covered with generic red balls that someone had bought in bulk at a discount store. *This* tree was very real and very crooked and loaded with an assortment of ornaments that must've come from decades' worth of holidays. Ones made from construction paper and popsicle sticks hung next to fancy, breakable decorations, and he had a feeling that each told its own story.

"Sorry, it looks like a tank battalion just stormed through here," Luke said, a piece of packing tape stuck to the side of his collar and a Nerf box tucked under his arm. "Merry Christmas and welcome to the war zone."

Isaac didn't think it was possible for his gut to clench any tighter, but it did at the potential double meaning behind Hannah's brother's comment. "Should I be expecting another battle from your sister tonight?"

"I'd put money on it if my mom and Sammy weren't here." Luke sighed. "Unfortunately, Hannah won't make a scene in front of either of them."

"Unfortunately?"

"Kylie and I were laying bets on how long it'd take for you guys to blow up at each other, but Carmen and Drew told us to knock it off and let you guys have space to talk things through. Then my dad chimed in and reminded us that she may not be willing to even talk to you." Luke lowered his voice conspiratorially. "I'm not allowed to tell you that we have a pool going, because it might tip the odds in my favor."

Great. Everybody was expecting Hannah to be upset that he was there. That wasn't exactly reassuring. "Does she know your mom invited me?"

"Nope."

"Don't you think she's going to be upset when she sees me here?"

"Hey, did you see our tree?" Luke gestured toward the middle of the room, his attempt to change the subject completely lacking even the pretense of subtlety. "The boys cut it down themselves a couple of days ago."

"Yeah, I was on the team responding to the 911 call

for the handsaw accident. How's Caden's finger doing, by the way?"

"Still attached, Chief." The boy in question held up a bandaged pinky covered in gauze. The cut hadn't been deep enough for stitches and one of the paramedics had easily cleaned it up and used a medical glue to close the wound. In Caden's other hand, he was holding up an extended box cutter. "Look, I found it, Dad. Aiden was using it to open the package of blaster darts."

Luke rolled his eyes, then took the dangerous tool out of his son's grasp. "As you may have noticed, we need to do a better job of keeping the boys away from sharp objects. Anyway, we have eggnog and cider and a full bar. If you could open this, I'll go grab you a drink."

Luke didn't wait for a response before passing over the box cutter and the Nerf soft dart launcher, still secured to its cardboard backing with impenetrable plastic ties. But having the task would give Isaac something to do other than wonder how Hannah might react when she saw him here.

He didn't have to wait long.

"What are you doing here?" Hannah asked from behind him as he struggled to free the toy and almost sliced through his own pinky.

"Your mom invited me." He turned around just in time to see her school the surprised expression on her face. Hopefully that meant she wasn't too upset. But just in case, he warned, "Apparently your family has a betting pool going on right now where we're concerned. So you might want to act like you're happy to see me or else Pop Pop is going to be sixty dollars ahead."

"I see they're upping the ante on their attempts to keep throwing us in each other's path." She was wearing a fuzzy green sweater and Isaac was glad his hands were otherwise occupied with freeing a toy from its bondage. Otherwise, he would've been tempted to reach his thumb out to test the soft, plush material. "Although, it seems you were a willing participant this time."

"In the interest of fairness, I was a willing participant for their last attempts, as well."

She jutted out her chin. "So you were fine with the bachelor auction?"

He shook his head. "God, no. I hated that. I was very unwilling for that one. But I wasn't reluctant about the outcome or being your date at the VFW."

Her brow creased. "And attending Luke and Carmen's wedding?"

"I had some reservations, but I'm a grown man. I could've easily said no on both occasions."

"Then why didn't you?" she asked.

Because he was a glutton for punishment and he wanted to be with Hannah any chance he got. Even if she hated him.

"Did you see the tree?" Isaac asked, using Luke's tactic to change the subject. "I sure hope they're keeping plenty of water in there. Fire hazard, you know."

"Luckily, my family seems to have a firefighter on speed dial." She managed a smirk before walking away. Just when he thought that she was going to dismiss him, she looked over her shoulder and added, "Come on. I think Sammy has a present for you buried under this mess somewhere."

Isaac felt a grin tug at the corners of his mouth and he followed her. As she drew him deeper into the heart of the room, deeper into the fold of her family, he let himself wonder if he could ever belong in her world. In a family like this.

Isaac scanned the room, his eyes landing on Sammy,

who had probably thought the same thing when he'd arrived from halfway across the globe to start a new life. But now Sammy was laughing with his new cousins, aiming squishy darts at a very unfortunate-looking snowman statue, and seeming to fit in perfectly.

If a six-year-old could do it, so could Isaac.

He gave a discreet cough and looked away when Hannah bent over to dig through some torn paper under the tree. Heat raced through him and he told himself that he was here for a family gathering and needed to stop lusting after his ex-girlfriend's curvy backside.

"Here it is," she called out, rising and waving a rectangular box wrapped in paper decorated with fire engines and wreaths. "We were going to bring it to the station after the holidays, but Sammy insisted all the gifts should go under the same tree. Sounds like he and my mom were in cahoots on getting you here tonight. I have no idea what's inside."

She stepped through a minefield of bows, a piece of bubble wrap attaching itself to her knee-high boots before she took a seat on an open spot of the gray suede sectional. "Sammy, do you want to give Chief Isaac your present?"

The boy looked over and, in his distraction, took a blunt-tipped orange dart to the temple.

"Sorry!" Aiden yelled.

But Sammy didn't seem to mind as he called out, "Cease fire," and made his way over toward his mom. Isaac was standing awkwardly beside the sofa when Sammy yanked on his arm.

"Sit here, next to Mama." Sammy all but shoved Isaac down onto the cushion beside Hannah before planting himself on the other side, preventing Isaac from scooting over. He could feel the heat radiating from her body as her legging-clad thigh pressed against his. It was way too warm and way too comfortable. Would it always have been this way if they hadn't held a grudge for so long? How many years had they wasted by not talking things out sooner?

And what could he do at this late date to rewrite history? Preferably, so that they could both come out on top.

Hannah had been livid two days ago when she found out her mother had gone AWOL and driven up the mountain road with Sammy and Big Dot to go to the fire station when she should've been resting. It was no wonder that Donna Gregson was able to shut down any further argument by declaring that she would feel more at peace if she knew her daughter was happy and had someone to love. And after that run-in with Elaine Marconi the same day, Hannah had resolved to try one more time to come to a resolution with Isaac. For nobody's sake but her own.

Of course, she hadn't expected that resolution to take place on Christmas Eve with her whole family eavesdropping.

Now Isaac was sitting beside her, the close proximity causing her pulse to skyrocket. He was holding Sammy's gift in his hand, turning it every which way as he studied the fire trucks on the paper and quizzed her son about which models they were. *Just open it, already. Before I spontaneously combust.*

For the past forty-eight hours, she'd desperately wanted to peek inside the package to see what her son had made for his hero. She was about to grab the gift herself and tear through the tape when Isaac finally slid his finger below a folded edge. It took forever—was he deliberately taking his time to neatly tear through Sammy's carefully taped seams?—but he eventually got to the plain white box underneath. By the time Isaac slowly lifted the lid, Hannah was wringing her hands in her lap.

The piles of red tissue paper took another thirty seconds to dig through and Hannah tapped her boot, frustrated that the only thing she could see under the tissue was the edge of a wooden frame.

"Did you make this yourself, big guy?" Isaac asked.

"Yep," her son said, sounding more and more like his American schoolmates. "Remember how I told you we drew pictures of our families in class? Well, when I was at the fire station, I didn't see a picture of *your* family in your office, so I drew one for you."

It took Hannah a moment to realize that Isaac was silent because he was, in fact, a bit overcome by Sammy's gift.

"I love it," Isaac said, a hint of emotion cracking through his good-time facade. When he wrapped an arm around Sammy's shoulders in a hug so intense even the boy seemed a bit surprised, Hannah leaned in for a closer look, but could only glimpse half of the portrait. It was clearly Isaac in his turnout gear, and the man with the bushy gray mustache beside him was his Uncle Jonesy. The fat, impossibly short-legged, speckled gray horse next to the man made it even more obvious that it was Isaac's uncle.

It wasn't until Isaac pulled away from Sammy that the box and tissue paper on his lap shifted, revealing the rest of the portrait. She gave a soft gasp when she realized that Sammy had drawn himself beside Isaac, the brown and tan colors blending where their hands were clasped. And then there was Hannah, her hair bright yellow and her head looking unusually large in comparison to the other people on the paper. Like, super large, with a cloud floating next to her oversize ear. The head and neck of

Big Dot (or possibly a cow) was squished in between Hannah's rounded kneecap and the edge of the page.

"I ran out of room here," Sammy said, pointing to the animal's front half. "I started drawing only you and Mr. Jonesy, because you guys are each other's family. But it was kinda plain and boring. I didn't know what your parents looked like, so I drew my mama in there 'cause she's a parent and you guys used to be best friends a long time ago."

Hannah's heart turned into a puddle inside her rib cage and she felt Isaac's shoulder move behind hers before his palm slid onto her back. "Good. Because I'd like to be best friends with your mama again."

"And then I had to squeeze me in right there because it's a family picture and me and Mama and Big Dot are a family and go together," Sammy said, and Hannah had to look up at the ceiling to keep the tears from spilling over onto her cheeks.

"Well, I think this family portrait is perfect and I can't wait to hang it in my office." Isaac's thumb traced circles against Hannah's lower spine, and for a few moments everything did, in fact, feel pretty perfect.

Then he smiled at her and her heart melted again. She should've known she would be a goner as soon as she walked into the pancake breakfast two months ago and saw him.

The doorbell rang, Big Dot barked and Sammy took off through a sea of toys and discarded gift wrap to chase the dog. Everyone else seemed to have moved toward the opposite end of the room, but Hannah and Isaac remained planted on the sofa, not saying a word. Was her family trying to give them space to talk? Or was someone hurt? Or were they watching a basketball game on TV? It really could be anything with her relatives.

Hannah leaned to the side, watching as Luke opened the front door to greet Jonesy with a laugh and a handshake. The two men looked over at Hannah and Isaac with a wink from her brother and a grouchy, "Well, what's takin' him so long?" from the older man before they slipped away into the kitchen.

"Looks like your uncle made the surprise guest list, too," she said when she turned back to Isaac. But instead of acknowledging her, he was holding the frame in his hands studying the drawing with a deep intensity that made Hannah's tummy flutter.

"Did you know about this?" Isaac finally asked.

"No clue. He brought it home that day my mom watched him. It was already wrapped."

She wanted to tell Isaac that he didn't have to actually hang the picture in his office. That it might be too awkward for him.

"What do you really think of the fa…of the portrait?" she asked, catching herself from saying *family* at the last minute.

"Well, it's not exactly accurate," he started, and Hannah felt the blood leave her face. Sammy was very proud of the drawing and would be hurt if Isaac totally disregarded it. But one side of Isaac's mouth curved up in a grin. "I mean, your head's not *literally* bigger than mine in real life and Uncle Jonesy is looking a bit thick in the midsection. He almost resembles Mayor Johnston."

A gurgle of laughter escaped from Hannah's lips, which had been clamped together, expecting the worst. Isaac continued, "And there's a few things I wouldn't mind adding."

Adding. Not subtracting.

"Like what?" Hannah held her breath.

"Like, Klondike needs her saddle and Big Dot needs

her red collar and this spot, right here, needs something." Isaac tapped on the glass over the uneven peach-colored ovals of Hannah's fingers on her left hand. "I'd draw a ring right here. Make it an official family portrait."

All the air left Hannah's lungs at once. She went light-headed. Did he just say what she thought he'd said?

She lifted her gaze to his, looking back and forth between his two eyes as though all the answers in the world could be found within those hazel depths.

"I know we hurt each other in the past," he said earnestly. "And I know you have Sammy and your mom's health and so many other things that you're dealing with right now. I'm not asking for a clean slate or to start over again, but you have to admit that there's something between us—some sort of connection—that we can't ignore. Deep down, Hannah, can you honestly tell me that we're not better when we're together?"

"I don't know. We've never been fully together. Like, all official, with none of that history weighing us down."

"I think we've been a lot more out in the open than either one of us would like to think."

"Small town gossip will always have its way of finding us," she warned. She'd made a resolution to no longer get sucked in by it, but that didn't mean they could avoid it.

"Well, yes, but it's not just gossip. Look at this portrait. Even Sammy can see that we're meant to be together. The other night you said that real love isn't guided by jealousy and jumping to conclusions. But it also isn't avoiding each other and leaving things unsaid. And who says that we need to continue to let those things guide us? Why can't we have a love that's guided by a mutual respect for each other's strengths and a shared joy in giving back to our community?"

He looked at Sammy, and then turned back to Hannah

and gently touched her cheek. "Why shouldn't we have a love based on our desire to paint our family portrait the way we want it to look?"

A ripple of longing spread through her. Hannah knew there were other people around them, but it felt as if they were the only two in the room. "Santa Baby" was playing somewhere in the background, but she could only hear Isaac's words. Pine branches and nutmeg and spiced cider surrounded them, but all she could smell was his aftershave—the same one he used to wear when they were young. She realized that it no longer mattered where they had this conversation, as long as they had it. Finally.

"Are you saying that you want to love me? To paint a family portrait with me?"

"Hannah, I do love you. I loved you way back then and I've had ten years now to realize that I never stopped. In fact, I probably love you even more right now because I already know what it's like to lose you. And, God help me, I don't want to lose you again."

"What about Sammy?" She knew Isaac cared about the boy, but her son needed stable, long-lasting influences in his life.

"Are you kidding?" Isaac's smile was huge. "I didn't need more than ten days to know that I don't want to lose him, either."

Her heart did somersaults and she used her chin to gesture toward where the dog was lapping up water from the tree stand. "And Big Dot?"

"I especially don't want to lose *her*. She's the only candidate for fire dog we have."

Hannah laughed. "I love you, too, Isaac Jones. You frustrate me and distract me and out-volunteer me every chance you get. But now that you're back in my life, I couldn't imagine it without you."

He smiled and leaned in as she wrapped her arms around his neck.

"They're kissing," Sammy yelled. "And we didn't even need the mistletoe, you guys!"

A loud cheer went up and Hannah knew that everyone had finally found their peace.

* * * * *

Look for the next book in
Christy Jeffries's miniseries Sugar Falls, Idaho,
The SEAL's Secret Daughter.
Available March 2019, wherever
Harlequin Special Edition books
and ebooks are sold.

COMING NEXT MONTH FROM

H HARLEQUIN®

SPECIAL EDITION

Available December 18, 2018

#2665 A DEAL MADE IN TEXAS
The Fortunes of Texas: The Lost Fortunes • by Michelle Major
It's like a scene from Christine Briscoe dreams when the flirtatious attorney asks her to be his (pretend) girlfriend. But there is nothing make-believe about the sparks between the quiet office manager and the sexy Fortune scion. Are they heading for heartbreak...or down the aisle?

#2666 THE COWBOY'S LESSON IN LOVE
Forever, Texas • by Marie Ferrarella
Ever since Clint Washburn's wife left, he's built up defenses to keep everyone in Forever out—including his son. Now the boy's teacher, Wynona Chee, is questioning his parenting! And Clint is experiencing feelings he thought long dead. Wynona has her homework cut out for her if she's going to teach this cowboy to love again.

#2667 A NEW LEASH ON LOVE
Furever Yours • by Melissa Senate
Army vet Matt Fielding is back home, figuring out his new normal. Goal one: find his niece the perfect puppy. He never expected to find the girl he'd left behind volunteering at the local shelter. Matt can't refuse Claire's offer of puppy training but will he be able to keep his emotional distance this time around?

#2668 THE LAWMAN'S CONVENIENT FAMILY
Rocking Chair Rodeo • by Judy Duarte
When Adam Santiago teams up with music therapist Julie Chapman to save two young orphans, pretty soon *his* heart's a goner, too! Julie's willing to do anything—even become Adam's pretend bride—to keep a brother and sister together. Will this marriage of convenience become an affair of the heart?

#2669 TWINS FOR THE SOLDIER
American Heroes • by Rochelle Alers
Army ranger Lee Remington didn't think he'd ever go back to Wickham Falls, home of some of his worst memories. But he's shocked by a powerful attraction to military widow Angela Mitchell. But as he preps for his ready-made family, there's one thing Lee forgot to tell her...

#2670 WINNING CHARLOTTE BACK
Sweet Briar Sweethearts • by Kathy Douglass
Dr. Rick Tyler just moved in next door to Charlotte Shields. She thought she'd seen the last of him when he abandoned her at the altar but he's determined to make the move work for his young son. Will he get a second chance with Charlotte in the bargain?

YOU CAN FIND MORE INFORMATION ON UPCOMING HARLEQUIN® TITLES, FREE EXCERPTS AND MORE AT WWW.HARLEQUIN.COM.

HSECNM1218

"Lisa," the man dressed as Zorro said, "I'd heard you were
going to be here."

He clearly thought Julie was someone else. She probably
ought to say something, but up close, the gorgeous bandito
seemed to have stolen both her thoughts and her words.

"It's nice to finally meet you." His deep voice set her senses
reeling. "I've never really liked blind dates."

Talk about masquerades and mistaken identities. Before
Julie could set him straight, he took her hand in a polished,
gentlemanly manner and kissed it. His warm breath lingered on
her skin, setting off a bevy of butterflies in her tummy.

"Dance with me," he said.

Her lips parted, but for the life of her, she still couldn't
speak, couldn't explain. And she darn sure couldn't object.

Zorro led her away from the buffet tables and to the dance
floor. When he opened his arms, she again had the opportunity
to tell him who she really was. But instead, she stepped into his
embrace, allowing him to take the lead.

His alluring aftershave, something manly, taunted her. As
she savored his scent, as well as the warmth of his muscular
arms, her pulse soared. She leaned her head on his shoulder

as they swayed to a sensual beat, their movements in perfect accord, as though they'd danced together a hundred times before.

Now would be a good time to tell him she wasn't Lisa, but she seemed to have fallen under a spell that grew stronger with every beat of the music. The moment turned surreal, like she'd stepped into a fairy tale with a handsome rogue.

Once again, she pondered revealing his mistake and telling him her name, but there'd be time enough to do that after the song ended. Then she'd return to the kitchen, slipping off like Cinderella. But instead of a glass slipper, she'd leave behind her momentary enchantment.

But several beats later, a cowboy tapped Zorro on the shoulder. "I need you to come outside."

Zorro looked at him and frowned. "Can't you see I'm busy?"

The cowboy, whose outfit was so authentic he seemed to be the real deal, rolled his eyes.

Julie wished she could have worn her street clothes. Would now be a good time to admit that she wasn't an actual attendee but here to work at the gala?

"What's up?" Zorro asked.

The cowboy folded his arms across his chest and shifted his weight to one hip. "Someone just broke into my pickup."

Zorro's gaze returned to Julie. "I'm sorry, Lisa. I'm going to have to morph into cop mode."

Now it was Julie's turn to tense. He was actually a police officer in real life? A slight uneasiness settled over her, an old habit she apparently hadn't outgrown. Not that she had any real reason to fear anyone in law enforcement nowadays.

Don't miss
The Lawman's Convenient Family *by Judy Duarte,*
available January 2019 wherever
Harlequin® Special Edition books and ebooks are sold.

www.Harlequin.com